Life Changing Journeys

TALES FROM THE WINDY CITY

CHICAGO

ADVENTURE

GREED

KIDNAPPING

SIBLING RIVALRY

SHARON MANGUM

LIFE CHANGING JOURNEYS
Tales from The Windy City

Sharon Mangum
seventaletrails@gmail.com

ISBN 978-1-943343-24-9

Printed in the United States of America
Destined To Publish
www.destinedtopublish.com

Dedication

In loving memory of my parents, Maydell and Warner Yokley. They inspired me and told me I could do anything I put my mind to, and I believed them.

CHICAGO

ADVENTURE

GREED

KIDNAPPING

SIBLING RIVALRY

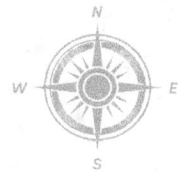

Acknowledgments

To my husband George, who always encouraged me to write, even when I thought I had nothing to say.

To my brother, Kevin, to whom I look for words of wisdom, wit, and humor. He has not disappointed me yet.

To Deborah and Kara, my writing coaches, who inspired me to reach beyond my limits.

CHICAGO

ADVENTURE

GREED

KIDNAPPING

SIBLING RIVALRY

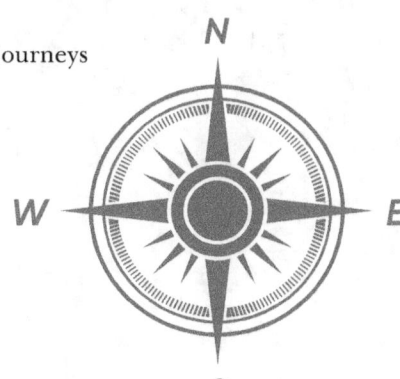

Contents

CHICAGO

ADVENTURE

GREED

KIDNAPPING

SIBLING RIVALRY

Introduction

This collection of tales is set mostly in Chicago. It is designed to entertain, teach, and provoke thought. The stories are told from the vantage points of multiple characters who are faced with dilemmas, from two brothers caught up in a sibling rivalry, kidnapped because of a laptop, to an aging matriarch fending off an attack by greedy relatives. Regardless of whether the challenge is physical, psychological, or one of moral turpitude, nothing is absolute and things are not always what they seem.

I invite you to take this journey and see whether, at the end of it, you have learned something or are provoked to a higher level of thought or, at the very least, entertained. You will experience kidnapping, drug smuggling, end-of-life issues, bullying, culinary culture, homelessness, and family greed. If you think you recognize any of the fictional characters in the book, this is a coincidence, but only speaks to the fact that we are more alike than we are different.

Dr. Hambrec's Revenge

CHICAGO

ADVENTURE

GREED

KIDNAPPING

SIBLING RIVALRY

Dr. Hambrec's Revenge

Jonathan and Geoffrie were as different as a moon and its eclipse. Although they were identical twins, Jonathan always seemed to be overshadowed in the presence of Geoffrie, and thus even strangers could tell them apart. They were six foot three, with an evenly distributed, muscular 190 pounds and dark brown, wavy hair. Though not decidedly handsome, they were attractive men who, given the right accessories and circumstances, could present themselves at such an advantage as to garner attention simply by entering a room. Geoffrie took full advantage of their physical attributes and played up every positive that could be manipulated. This included choosing the right color scheme to complement his smooth, chocolate brown complexion and went right down to maintaining well-manicured hands that hinted at his pride in his surgical skills. Jonathan, on the other hand, dressed practically. He didn't care if his clothing was coordinated as long as it was clean and reasonably free of wrinkles.

Growing up on the south side of Chicago, Geoffrie had always been Jonathan's protector and felt that he was the main reason J was the success he had come to be. J was the nickname Geoffrie had for Jonathan, and he often employed it when he felt the kindred bond that only brothers experience—the kind of bond that allowed them to look across a room and relay a thought or idea with visual contact. Yes, Geoffrie even thought J was less than equipped to deal with a lot of the harsh realities of life and, likewise, medicine. What Geoffrie didn't know was that J had his own inner strength, which had allowed him to endure the indignity of always being compared to his brother and taking a backseat to Geoffrie without thinking less of himself.

Geoffrie always thought he had convinced J to apply to medical school with him, but he had never allowed himself to consider that his brother had always wanted to be a doctor. This desire may have been fostered by their father, who was a veterinarian and maintained that it was better than being a medical doctor. After all, he said, his patients had no need to dump their personal problems on him or complain about their in-laws, as often occurs with their human counterparts. Despite his good-natured ribbing, they both knew he was proud of "my son, the surgeon" and "my boy, the internist," as he often called them when bragging to his friends.

Their mother, equally proud, had given up a career as a family practitioner in a busy downtown office that was affiliated with one of the major teaching institutions in Chicago. She felt it was more important to raise decent sons and productive citizens than to amass a small fortune. Although not affluent, living on the single salary of their father, they did not starve. They lived a nice, quiet existence that J had treasured and tried to sustain into his own adult years. And yet the events of the past forty-eight hours threatened to destroy his serene little world and force him out of his comfort zone.

He would have to rely on the inner strength that most people didn't know he had and that Geoffrie had never dreamed existed. And, most importantly, Geoffrie's very life depended on a brother he had underestimated for the better part of forty-three years.

On September 14, 2000, Geoffrie woke up ready to start what appeared to be a very promising day. However, first things first: he needed to let Quinn know that he hadn't meant to leave her stuck with the bill for their elaborate meal at Chez Charrise. He realized he had to apologize, but the urgent call he received from Germany more than made up for the anger he was prepared to face from his fiancé. After all, it wasn't as if she didn't have his American Express card to charge the two hundred dollars to. The meal was sumptuous, including the escargot appetizer and the grand finale of the richest chocolate mousse cake he had ever tasted. But right in the middle of his cappuccino, the nagging ringer of his cell phone warned him that the evening would not be a quiet one. Taking out his cell phone, he saw a number that was not at all familiar to him, but he knew enough about the area code to surmise that it was an international call.

The voice on the other end, heavily accented, inquired, "Is this Dr. Geoffrie Stein?"

Somewhat cautious despite his international fame, Geoffrie replied, "Yes, it is, and to whom am I speaking?"

"I am Dr. Franc Hambrec. I was given your number by a mutual colleague who felt that you might be interested in collaborating on a research project that would make special use of your talent and current interest!" The voice on the other end sounded very excited and somewhat breathless. However, before Geoffrie could respond, the voice advised him that no further details could be given over the phone due to security concerns.

"How can I get in touch with you?" Geoffrie replied, half thinking that this might be a dim-witted joke from some of his alpha frat brothers.

"Go home immediately!" the breathless voice continued, "and log on to your computer and check your email. Follow the instructions in the message from greedybaby at international. com."

Geoffrie started to interrupt. "How did you get my email—"

"Waste no time!" The voice was getting impatient. "If you do not download the message within one hour, it will automatically self-delete from your email inbox."

Geoffrie immediately jumped up and, much to Quinn's surprise, started running to the exit, tripping as he went over unsuspecting customers, who were trying to enjoy a leisurely meal. "Sorry, sweetheart! This is urgent! I'll call you later." The words trailed behind him as he stumbled out the door.

Breathless and panting after running up the stairs to his brownstone in Dearborn Park, Geoffrie turned the key in the knob to his front door and went straight to the study. In his haste, he didn't notice that there was no click when he turned the key and his alarm was not on—that is, until he reached the study. *The computer was gone!* He went back and checked the front door. Sure enough, the lock had been forced.

After checking to make sure nothing else was missing, he called the police and filed a report. However, he felt as if it was a waste of time. Whoever had ripped him off was very proficient at breaking and entering and had left little, if any, evidence. He was sure there would be no prints from the police dustings.

Angry and disappointed, but with heightened interest, Geoffrie prepared for bed. His thoughts were racing. What could this series of events be related to?

The call from "Dr. Hambrec" spoke of his special interests, but his most recent project had reached a dead end. He continued to mentally scan all the research projects he had recently completed or consulted on, and none of them seemed to be of any particular significance that would warrant someone breaking and entering his home. Geoffrie subsequently fell asleep, forgetting his promise to call Quinn.

* * * * * * *

Fueled by the excitement of the previous night, Geoffrie refocused and dialed Quinn's number.

"Hello?" a very sultry but casual voice queried.

"I'm sorry!" Geoffrie blurted out.

"Wait a minute! You don't bother to say hello anymore?"

"I'm trying to get my plea in before you put me on your S-list."

"Why would I delete you from my social calendar? After all, I've only been stood up five to six times in the past year I've known you. Plus you've left me stranded with an outlandish bill an equal number of times. But this time, I at least had your credit card from our last date."

Geoffrie now recalled giving Quinn his American Express card to buy "something nice" to make up for the last interrupted date. He hadn't gotten it back, and up until now hadn't missed it. He wasn't sure Quinn was kidding until he heard her light, effervescent laugh (which always reminded him of wind chimes).

"Come on, Geoff. It isn't all that serious. Besides, you usually have a good reason. So I'm very curious to find out what last night was about."

Geoffrie advised her of the mysterious call. He left out the fact that someone had broken into his condominium, not wanting to worry her. He breathed a sigh of relief, realizing that outside of his work and family, his relationship with Quinn was the only thing of real value to him. If you asked Geoffrie's friends what was important to him, they would guess that it was his job first, his jet-black Porsche second, and his family and Quinn running a distant third. What they didn't know about Geoffrie was that the things he talked about the least were the most important to him (i.e., his family and Quinn). Geoffrie learned early in life that his priorities were potential tools for use by others to manipulate him. His choice topics of conversation were his job and car, leaving his friends to feel that he was materially centered. The fact that he only wore the best of clothing and ate the best of food only reinforced their notion that he was a self- centered son of a biscuit.

However, most of them forgave what they perceived as selfishness and arrogance because of his charm. Quinn was the only one he had allowed to get beyond the layers and years of psychological armor to see the real Geoffrie. Even J wasn't allowed an in-depth view of Geoffrie's persona. Geoffrie was afraid that if J knew his fears and vulnerabilities, J would no longer feel protected by his "older" brother. (Geoffrie was older than J by two minutes). His parents were, by far, the people who best knew and understood him. Quinn was slowly growing in the same knowledge.

As Quinn continued to forgive Geoffrie, he heard the chimes of his front door. Without thinking, he shouted, "Come on in!" The lock was still broken from the night before and he hadn't time to replace it yet.

"Hey, man! Since when have you been leaving your door unlocked?" J sauntered in with his usual casual air.

"Hold on, old man! I'll be right with you. I'm on the phone with Quinn."

"Hey, give her my love!" J was hesitant in his choice of words since he always felt that Geoffrie had stolen Quinn right out from under his nose while he was dating her.

"Quinn, baby, let me catch you later. Can we maybe try dinner again?"

"Only if it's at my house! That way, if you get any more mysterious calls, I won't be embarrassed by your running out on me. Honestly, Geoffrie, people must have thought I had threatened your life, the way you fled!" Again, this was followed by Quinn's lighthearted laugh and Geoff knew he was forgiven.

He then decided she was absolutely wonderful and his previous two marriages were just training until he found the "real meal deal." Quinn was as real as they come.

J, seeing the smile on Geoffrie's face as he hung up, knew that if this man was not his flesh and blood, he would probably have harbored a fierce hate for him. After all, J saw her first.

Quinn and J had met at a medical conference. Although Quinn had given up practicing medicine to teach high school math, she kept her license active and stayed abreast of all medical advances. J had spotted her in the sea of professionals because she was so "real." She didn't hide behind tons of cosmetics, false hair, and overpriced clothing, as was the custom of some female doctors that "J" had met during his career. Her wavy black hair was pulled back in a ponytail that was tamed by hairpins holding it in place. The most striking feature of her face were the biggest brown eyes he had ever imagined and a depth that he felt he could pleasantly drown in. She wore a simple white sleeveless silk shell with a straight black skirt, which was also probably silk. Although she was only five foot three, she wore flats. J was impressed by her simple dress and demure composure. Many women of small stature, he found, often wore heels to professional events to appear more imposing or important, or so he thought. Quinn, however, was a woman of stature despite her size. Her intelligence and poise raised her head and shoulders above all the other doctors he had conversed with at the conference.

Having met and clicked at a physician's conference in Philadelphia, they agreed to meet again when they returned to Chicago. Wonder of wonders that he should go away to Philadelphia to meet the "perfect woman" when she was living right under his nose, here in Chicago.

Their first date was so charged with excitement on J's part that he actually went out and bought brand-new clothes.

Not trusting his own taste, he invited Geoffrie to help him shop. That was his first mistake. Geoffrie insisted on meeting the woman that could inspire his little brother to make a fashion statement. J advised him that he could only stop by their table for a few minutes at the restaurant. Even then, he wanted Geoffrie to pretend he just happened to be at the same restaurant. He didn't want Quinn to feel as if she was undergoing inspection.

Well, when Geoffrie arrived and met Quinn, he stayed more than a few minutes. He stayed for the entire meal and ate a five-course dinner. During this ordeal, not only did he monopolize the conversation, but he proceeded to embarrass J by telling Quinn about the special preparation that he had made for this date, including the shopping trip. Whoever said "All is fair in love and war" had never met Geoffrie! But J couldn't blame everything on Geoffrie since Quinn, who was initially intrigued by the fact that they were identical twins, soon directed all of her attention to Geoffrie.

At the end of the date, Geoffrie asked Quinn out again.

Being diplomatic, she stated, "I would just love to be in the company of such handsome escorts again!"

However, J knew any subsequent encounters with the three of them would only mean humiliation for him since he was no longer the object of her attention. And the rest, as they say, is history.

J, unlike Geoffrie, had never been married and had been questioned several times about why. The simple fact of the matter was that he was more selective than Geoffrie (by his viewpoint) and felt no need to waste time developing relationships with women unless they were people he could potentially build a life with.

Quinn had also never been married, but at age forty-five, she could still pass for thirty and never felt compelled to explain what she saw as obvious. The obvious to her was that she was strong, independent, and financially secure and was not going to get hitched just to satisfy society's notion of what she should be. J felt this was a definite plus and knew that whenever and however this woman married, it would be for life (and for love).

She was also very talented, a classically trained pianist. With great hopes that she would pursue a musical career, her parents had bought her a piano at age ten. It was the best Steinway they could afford on a middle-class salary. They were proud that it was brand-new. Often her parents bought used or secondhand items to save money, but the future of their only daughter was not something they were going to scrimp on.

After many recitals and junior competitions, Quinn found that she was happy just playing for her own pleasure and relaxation. So when she decided to go to medical school, she paid her own way with loans and by doing minor clothing alterations on the side. She never wanted to feel indebted or guilty for making career choices that could affect the rest of her life.

J's thoughts quickly returned to the present as Geoffrie put down his cell.

"Okay, Geoff, let's get out of here before we lose our reservation at the racquetball court!" Saturdays were always booked solid, and if you were even ten minutes late, you would forfeit your slot.

10

"Can't go. I have to get the lock changed on my door. "

"Why? What for?"

Geoffrie explained the events of the night before. J was absolutely appalled, but felt that Geoffrie lived his life in a fish bowl and somewhat invited this type of notoriety. These thoughts he kept to himself. Little did J know that these events would soon engulf and carry him along for the ride, too.

"Well, unless you need me to help, I'm going to shove off." J could think of more exciting ways to spend his Saturday, and they didn't include doing handyman chores around the house. After all, how many doctors did it take to change a lock? In this case, three—he and Geoffrie to watch and the third to call the locksmith. Neither he nor Geoffrie was manually inclined outside of the operating room, or the office. Unlike Geoffrie, J readily admitted it. Curious about this Dr. Hambrec, J stopped off at his office to check the international directory of doctors to see what background he could obtain on "the voice." As he continued his investigation on the internet, he found there was no person by the name of Franc Hambrec listed. Well, that figures, he thought. Who would use their real name if they were involved in schemes like breaking and entering and theft? But J knew there was more to the puzzle than the theft of a computer since none of Geoffrie's other valuables were touched, including his rare coin collection.

J, who didn't like to take his work home, used Geoffrie's computer when he didn't feel like driving to the office. Now, with Geoffrie's computer gone, he would have to continue work on his latest project at the office. Fortunately, he had backup files for his data, and he proceeded to load these into his computer. J pulled up the program he needed and plugged

11

in the data from his experiments the day before. He was so excited about this project that his everyday practice of seeing patients was beginning to seem mundane in comparison. It was a surprisingly simple concept that could revolutionize the practice of medicine and put a whole new face on aging.

After sitting at the computer for almost eight hours, he needed a serious break. He thought he would go home, shower, check his messages, and maybe go to a movie with a friend. He considered calling Danielle, but he hadn't spoken with her in months and didn't feel up to the 411 on the latest "excitement" in her life. That woman could put a rock to sleep.

Arriving in Lincoln Park, as usual, he had problems finding a place to park. Fortunately, his car was nine years old and he could park it anywhere without fear of theft. If it was towed, he would simply leave it at the pound and have it sold for scrap. Unlike, his last girlfriend, who named her cars as if they were people or pets, he had no emotional attachment to his Maxima.

Upon walking the block to his townhouse, J began to turn over in his mind everything that had happened to Geoffrie in the last twenty-four hours. Wow! he thought, I sure hope Geoff has nine lives, because he's certainly living close to the edge these days. J was calling to mind the many things Geoffrie had done and tried in the past "just because." To name a few of his ventures, most of which were based on bets or dares, he had walked a tightrope thirty feet above the ground without a net (at a local fair), skydived, bungee-jumped, tried fire-eating, juggled torches, and just about anything else that wasn't fattening, immoral, or elicit. But he had never been involved in any activity that was so ominous it would necessitate someone

12

breaking into his house. Geoffrie had assured J that he was not mixed up in anything illegal, and J believed him!

Whoever this Hambrec was, he would undoubtedly surface again. But what did he need Geoffrie's computer for, if he was the one who stole it? All of Geoffrie's research projects and data were kept on a new device called Datatrex (the latest in research data storage). It operates pretty much the same as a computer, but will not allow access to files, data, or programs without checking the user's DNA to see if it matches the owner's. This is done by a finger stick that elicits one drop of blood, so small, it can not be seen by the human eye (containing one to two red blood cells). Datatrex rapidly analyzes the DNA, if it is a match, the user is given complete access to all of its contents and functions. If it's not a match, Datatrex will deliver a shock to the user's finger, strong enough to render him unconscious for thirty minutes. All of this takes place in microseconds, so if you are not the owner, the shock you receive will be instantaneous after placing a finger in the user port. If the intruder is brave enough to try again, the next shock will deliver enough energy to cause soft tissue damage in the muscles and mild renal failure. Anyone still strong enough and stupid enough to try a third time will receive enough energy to stop the heart!

With this new device, Geoffrie was no longer concerned about hackers, either. The Datatrex was designed to automatically track anyone trying to break into the system electronically. Hardware of a hacker's computer would be destroyed by an army of computer viruses sent back across the same line that the hacker used to attempt to gain access.

The system was conceived, created, and perfected by none other than the eminent Dr. Geoffrie Stein. The patent alone was valued in millions of dollars, with the prototype locked away in Geoffrie's research lab. Several systems had been built and were being used in government labs around the country. Only Geoffrie, J, and top military personnel knew of its existence. With this new technology, Geoffrie used his regular computer only for games and recreation.

Although Geoffrie encouraged J to store his data on Geoffrie's Datatrex, J was leery of the prospect of being shocked. He knew he was being silly, since Geoff had programed datatrex, to recognize his DNA, as well as, Geoff's, which was only slightly different, being identical twins. Still he didn't relish the idea of being toast. J also didn't feel that his projects were worthy of such protection and regularly downplayed their importance. That is, until his latest project. He had planned to tell Geoffrie about it today, but forgot after they didn't play racquetball.

For a second after realizing his data was on Geoffrie's computer, which had been stolen the previous night, J panicked. The living room of his spacious townhome started to close in. A wave of nausea rose in his throat as his heart raced violently. His visual field started to narrow.

Then he heard an inner voice: "Get a hold of yourself, man! You thought something like this was possible, and that's why you only placed half of the project on Geoffrie's computer. One half is no good without the other!" Any hacker would also have to figure out his password. That should slow them down and buy him some time to figure out what was going on. J now began to consider the possibility that maybe he was more involved in this mystery than he'd originally thought.

Sitting down to steady his nerves, J glanced at his messages and recognized Quinn's number on his caller ID.

Quinn's calls were few and far between since she'd become engaged to Geoffrie, so his curiosity prompted him to return her call first.

Pulling up her number, from the remote memory on his cell, he briefly reflected on what might have been. Quinn, who was usually calm, sounded perplexed as she explained to J that Geoffrie didn't show up for their dinner date. It was now 10:00 p.m. Geoffrie was always late, but would at least call to let her know he wouldn't be on time.

After reassuring her, J called Geoffrie. When he heard the voicemail kick in, he decided to drive to Geoffrie's place.

The door was standing wide open! J stepped inside, pulling together every ounce of courage he had, but feeling like the doomed victim in a cheap horror flick. As he advanced, he began to take inventory of the damage that had been done.

Unlike, the previous intruder, this one clearly hadn't known what to look for and hence tore up the whole house. One pattern was still unchanged: they hadn't taken anything of obvious value. Geoffrie's diamond cuff links and tie clip were untouched; the rare coin collection was still in its mounted glass over the fireplace; the vintage VCR player, stereo, and big-screen TV were all intact. At this point, J was convinced that they were looking for information, the kind that's worth far more than the valuables they'd ignored in Geoffrie's living room. Suddenly J realized he still hadn't located Geoffrie. Running through the house calling his brother's name he realized he wasn't there. J then went to the garage and found the Porsche gone. J hoped and prayed with all his heart that Geoffrie and his car were together and intact.

Minutes after J called the police, they were there, dusting for prints and asking the usual questions in reference to potential enemies of the victim, threats against the victim, etc. J knew their approach was all wrong for this type of crime. This was impersonal, the victim was not the objective, something of intangible value was the target of this series of break-ins, and Geoffrie just happened to be the key to whatever these people were after. With no leads, and the police treating the crime as a kidnapping despite the absence of a ransom note and a million dollars' worth of merchandise left untouched in an unlocked house, J knew he would have to locate Geoffrie on his own. He just hoped he wasn't too late!

After some quick thinking, J decided the only way to find Geoffrie, and find out what these people wanted, was to take his place. He had to convince them they had the wrong Dr. Stein, provided Geoffrie was still alive. Well, at least there was no blood at the house. He started to call Quinn and advise her of his plan. Then he reconsidered this decision.

In order for him to pass as Geoffrie, everyone close to him would have to treat him like Geoffrie. But Quinn wouldn't be able to treat J exactly as she treated Geoffrie because of her emotional attachment and loyalty, even with Geoffrie's life depending on it. Therefore he felt justified in not telling her and hoped she wouldn't hate him later. Was he taking advantage of a bad situation? He hoped not!

With all the charm and charisma he could gather, he called Quinn and pretended to be Geoffrie. He told her he'd had a minor car accident and was unable to call her because his cell phone was destroyed after it was thrown from the car in the collision, but that he was okay.

16

"Geoffrie, are you sure you're okay? You sound different . . . serious." Quinn sounded more concerned than suspicious. But J knew that if he was going to pull this off, he would have to get a lot better at being more of the moon and less of the eclipse, and quickly! He assured her again, as Geoffrie would have, and promised to make it up to her by taking her to Mackinaw Island during her next vacation break. In the meantime, he told her that J had just left and was going away for a few days for some rest and relaxation.

"That's rather sudden. I just sent him over there to check on you several hours ago."

"Yeah, he was here. We played a few games of chess and then he shoved off. I told him I would call you myself and repent of my errant ways! After all, I can't have you kibitzing too much with your old flame. He might rekindle some sparks." J felt as if he was getting better with each lie.

Quinn laughed and he imagined her dark brown eyes twinkling in the night, like pools of water reflecting the essence of the stars.

"Quinn, I hate to ask you, but do you think you could help me by seeing walk-ins at his office for the next three or so days? I realize you'll be going back to teaching in two weeks and this cuts into your vacation, but I'll be lecturing next week and I'll need to prepare slides and continue with my research project." J actually needed the extra time to find Geoffrie and convince the medical community that he was still present, thereby convincing his captors that they had the wrong Dr. Stein and forcing their hand so they would come after him.

"Sure, Geoff. Just don't stand me up anymore this week. With everything that's happened, I'm afraid you're going to

17

come up missing!" Quinn laughed, but it wasn't her usual light fare. It was nervous and somewhat sad.

In that fleeting moment, J both hated himself for deceiving Quinn and pitied himself for not putting up a fight when Geoffrie stole her away from him. That was his second mistake. After he allowed Geoffrie to meet Quinn, he offered no resistance to him wooing his date, on his time and money. No wonder Quinn paid little attention to him the remainder of the date. It was as if he wasn't there. J was beginning to realize that some things have to be competed for if they're worth having.

With that realization, J bade Quinn goodnight with all the romantic fanfare he imagined Geoffrie would, and began to clean up "his house."

J was reorganizing Geoffrie's CDs when he found his favorite classic rock album "Frampton Comes Alive", by Peter Frampton. He and Geoffrie seemed to have the same tastes in music and, recently, women. As he continued cleaning, he played *various albums that he had grown up listening to and marvelled that* Geoffrie's collection was almost identical to his. Yes, he and Geoffrie were both "rock heads" and "funk fans." He even recalled the time Geoffrie wanted classic rock piped into the OR while he performed his surgeries. The head of the Department of Surgery, at that time, advised Geoffrie that the likes of rock, classic or otherwise, would only be heard in the ORs of St. Barrister's Hospital when hell froze over. Well, sometime between that conversation and Geoffrie's ascension to head of the surgical department, there must have been a deep freeze. Now, every Wednesday and Friday between 7:00 a.m. and noon, strains of various rock artists and "Parliament" (a famous funk group from the 1960s and on) could be heard coming from OR-8, the operating room reserved for Geoffrie's cases. Geoffrie had even considered piping in rap, but thought better of it. St. Barrie's wasn't quite ready for Rap yet.

This Wednesday and Friday would be different! J wasn't prepared to take over Geoffrie's surgical cases and thus would cancel all the elective cases and ask Dr. Ben Kasey to cover the emergencies. "No kidding, this guy's name really is Ben Kasey," Geoffrie had said when he'd first introduced the surgeon to J. It was as if his parents had played a bad joke on him, and becoming anything other than a doctor would have labeled him a failure. Ben took it all in stride, but had to remind people that "Kasey" was spelled with a "K", not a "C". Ben Casey was a popular TV doctor from the 1960's.

After calling Ben and arranging surgical coverage, J began to plan his strategy for assuming Geoffrie's identity and unraveling the mystery.

* * * * * * *

Geoffrie came to with the worst headache he'd ever had. The last thing he remembered was sliding across three lanes of traffic on Lake Shore Drive, and then a crash and a sickening thud. That thud was his car diving into the depths of Lake Michigan. With barely enough time to think, he quickly rolled down the window. As the water came in, he swam out through the window.

Pulling himself up on the rocks, he could see the lights from a burgundy SUV—the same SUV that had been parked three doors down from his house for about a week now. He had been racing to get to J's place to tell him he'd latched onto something that might explain the theft of his computer. He'd been so excited that he had left straight from the hardware store without stopping at home to fix his lock. He hadn't noticed the

SUV while at the hardware store, but it must have been there, because it immediately picked up his trail soon after he left. Initially he'd tried to convince himself that this wasn't the same van he had seen outside his house. However, when he realized the SUV was making the same lane changes he was, he knew he was being followed.

Gasping for breath, Geoffrie could see figures emerge from the SUV. With the fight-or-flight instinct of a hunted animal, Geoffrie pulled himself up to his knees and then his feet. The rush of adrenaline and fear propelled him upward and into the night with such force and speed, he hardly noticed the pain in his left side. Stumbling as he went and looking back, he noticed the figures were not in pursuit. Soon, to his dismay, he realized something else was coming after him. As it gained ground, Geoffrie could see fierce, wild eyes and white fang-like teeth. "Oh, my goodness! They've got a raging pit bull chasing me!"

As Geoffrie tried to escape, he fell and hit his head. He heard one of them say, "Hold short, Riff!" Just then, Geoffrie lost consciousness with Riff's teeth inches from his neck.

Coming to, Geoffrie realized he was in a hospital. Maybe he had been rescued from his captors. He surveyed his surroundings, but realized he could only see the part of the room that was immediately in front of him. He tried to turn his neck, but couldn't. Then he tried to move his arms and legs. "Oh, my God, I'm paralyzed!" he tried to scream, but no sound left his mouth.

Just at that instant of terror, a familiar voice said, "Don't worry, Dr. Stein. Your paralysis is only temporary—that is, if you cooperate."

Geoffrie recognized the voice of "Dr. Hambrec," or whatever he was calling himself these days. As someone approached the bed and entered his view, Geoffrie saw that the voice was coming from a figure of perhaps only five foot four, with shoulder-length blonde hair, green eyes, and a silhouette that would have put a pageant queen to shame. Although the raspy voice was only one or two octaves higher than a bass, Geoffrie knew a lady when he saw one.

"Don't stare, unless you want to lose your eyesight as well!" the raspy, accented voice continued. "You, Dr. Stein, like all elitist pig doctors, think I'm a freak. Well, I'm not! I'm just one of many surgical procedures gone wrong."

Geoffrie listened intently, not out of interest in this woman's personal plight, but because the balance of his life was in her hands. Therefore he listened to a short narrative that could have been set to violin music.

Walking from one side of his bed to the other for emphasis, she continued. "Once, I had a beautiful operatic voice. When I developed nodules on my vocal cords, I was told I should have them removed if I wanted to continue my career. So I agreed. Hours after the procedure, this was all that was left of my talent. So, you see, I'm not a product of nature, but of bad medicine. I've been deprived of fame and fortune. And although I can't have fame, you are going to help me get my fortune. "

Finding his voice after recovering from the shock of not being able to move, Geoffrie wondered aloud, "But how can I help you? Is this a kidnapping?"

"Oh, don't be so stupid! Your personal worth has limits, but this latest project you're working on has the potential

21

for endless millions!" Immediately, after she finished her statement, Geoffrie felt a blinding blow land on his left jaw. It was so sharp, it took his breath away! At that moment, he realized there were three other people in the room. The fist that had just punched him belonged to a big, burly man about six foot eight, weighing in at 300 pounds. Another was a man of a more average build at five foot eleven and 180 pounds. Lastly, was an individual who was about 5 foot 3 inches, and 130 pounds. Together, they comprised the group that had hunted him down with the "rabid" pit bull.

Before the captive could recover completely from what he felt was unsolicited punishment, Dr. Hambrec explained, "You're supposed to be one of the smartest men in your field, so every time you ask a stupid question or make a stupid statement, you will elicit a consequence. It won't always be the same, but it will always be either very painful or very unpleasant. And the unfortunate part for you is that you can't defend against it. Therefore, Dr. Stein, if I were you, I would choose my words very carefully."

At this moment, Geoffrie wondered where the vicious dog was and what role he would play in this torture.

Dr. Hambrec, who wasn't really a doctor, continued. "I have part of a project that my associate found on your computer after he hacked his way in. You see, I've been searching for years to see if my voice could be restored by the very people who destroyed it. I have gone to many doctors and many conferences, but going online and learning about you was the smartest thing I've done since that unfortunate event. I decided that if I followed your career long enough, you would come up with something useful for people like me. So I hired Mr. Max, an expert computer hacker, to break into your system."

22

With this revelation, Geoffrie surveyed the smallest of the group, assuming that he must be Mr. Max, since he clearly was not recruited for braun. J decided he'd seen wet noodles that looked more intelligent.

The deranged kidnapper continued. "But you've disappointed me; you have done no research in this area. However, you have been working on another project, which won't help my voice, but could make me rich."

Geoffrie had absolutely no idea what this delusional woman was talking about; and for the first time in this forty-eight-hour ordeal, he was beginning to feel hopeless. Actually, it was more than forty-eight hours. He knew this because the big, dumb burly one had just flung a newspaper in his lap.

"What the hell is this? the big burly man demanded. Much to Geoffrie's surprise, a picture of J at a fundraiser at the Glass Top Heston Hotel appeared on the Society page. The caption read, "The eminent and extremely eligible Dr. Geoffrie Stein participated in a bachelor auction at the Glass Top last night in the presence of other successful Chicago-area bachelors."

Who knew It could read? Geoffrie chuckled to himself as he surveyed the hairy creature that had just placed this tidbit of news within his visual field. Amid all of the excitement, Geoffrie had forgotten about his social obligations. But somehow, as much as J hated these fundraisers, he had sucked it up long enough to make an appearance (impersonating Geoffrie). At this point, Geoffrie realized that J must have a plan! Why else would he suffer through what would otherwise be an intolerable evening for him?

Dr. Hambrec walked over, looked at the picture, and belted out a deep, throaty laugh. "I knew he had a twin, but trust me, we've got our man. And I'm going to get the other half of Super Cell."

"Super Cell?" Geoffrie thought it sounded like the title of some B-rated sci-fi flick. As he laid there, it finally occurred to him that J had been using his computer for more than just games. He had actually put something important on Geoffrie's computer without his knowledge. Crap! He had tried to convince J to use his Datatrex for all of his important work. Now he might very well have to die for J's indiscretion. He wouldn't call it stupidity, because J was anything but stupid. However, Geoffrie could never understand why J wouldn't use Datatrex. It was certainly more secure than any computer. This latest series of events could attest to that.

Well, for now, Geoffrie would at least need to pretend that he knew what they were talking about in order to stay alive. As soon as they realized they really did have the wrong Stein (as in the one who didn't know diddly about Super Cell), he could forget about ever seeing Quinn again.

Speaking of which, he wondered how she was coping with his disappearance. Probably a nervous wreck, he supposed.

Just then, Hambrec interrupted his thoughts. "Back to the business at hand, Bacon Head! Where is the other half of Super Cell? You can tell me now and spare yourself some grief, or we can go through the whole program of entertainment that I have planned for you."

"Why is this data of any importance to you?" Geoffrie knew he risked being punched again, or something worse. To his surprise, there was no consequence.

Hambrec smiled. "This brilliant concept that you have come up with in genetic engineering is the virtual fountain of youth!"

The project that J had been working on for five years involved changing the genetic code of one type of cell so the gene that would cause it to eventually age and die was turned off. In its place, he had inserted a new gene that would cause the cell to replicate and overtake any normal cell of the same tissue type. In a sense, the new, energized cell was like a cancer, except that the tissue was of normal function and morphology. When all the old cells were replaced by the super cell line, the gene would be turned off by the absence of further "prey." A whole new kidney, heart, lung, or other organ would be left in place of the old organ and would never age or die. With this technology, transplants would no longer be needed as long as one donor super cell could be found that was a compatible tissue match, with the recipient. Further into the future, a young adult or teenager could have cells taken from all of their organs and frozen for future "superization." These cells could be held in reserve and, when needed, injected into the old organ to get a completely new functioning organ.

This would eliminate the need for surgery, donors, or artificial organs. One super cell could be inserted into the patient's organ with a needle, depending on the location of the organ to be replaced. Also, depending on the size of the organ, the process could be completed in as little as a week.

So far, J had only completed successful testing on small mammals like hamsters. There was still a lot to be done, but he was ready to print and present his preliminary data—until Geoffrie's computer was stolen.

What Hambrec had in mind was to start a transplant clinic and charge people for transplanted organs and surgeries that they weren't getting. In essence, she would set up OR time, take the patient to surgery, make an incision, and implant the super cell in a matter of minutes. Then she would charge for a major surgery, a donor organ, and hours of OR time and anesthesia.

* * * * * * *

The police had called J's apartment earlier in the day and still had no leads. They did find a witness who saw a car matching the description of Geoffrie's Porsche jump the embankment of LSD (Lake Shore Drive) and fly into Lake Michigan. The witness didn't see much else since they were driving along in traffic. To this end, the police were now dragging the lake, looking for Geoffrie's car and any sign of the owner. This bit of news sent a chill down J's spine, and for the first time he began to wonder if he would ever see Geoffrie alive again! He had asked the police to keep Geoffrie's disappearance out of the media and, much to his surprise, they had complied.

In preparation for his first lecture as Dr. Geoffrie Stein, J decided to review Geoffrie's notes again. Therefore, he had to drive back to Geoffrie's lab. When he arrived, he had the eerie feeling that he was being watched. However, so much had happened lately that J thought he was just a little paranoid.

As he initiated entry to Geoffrie's files, he heard a creaking noise in the hallway. J quickly disengaged Datatrex and switched off the light. In that instance, the door flew open and a dark figure tackled him and pinned him to the floor.

"What do you want?" J gasped as he tried to pry the stranger's fingers from around his neck.

"Shut up! I'll do the talking!" The figure dragged him to a chair. While holding a gun to his head, the figure switched on the nearest light with his free hand. As J's eyes adjusted to the light, he saw a muscular man in a black ski mask and sweats.

"Turn it back on!" the gruff voice snarled, pointing to the Datatrex.

"You turn it on!" J taunted. He then heard the man ready his gun. J held his breath. After seconds, which seemed like minutes, the intruder removed the gun from his head.

"Look, I have the gun! So even though I won't kill you until I get what I want, I will hurt you! So you better cooperate!" The stranger pointed the gun at J's face for emphasis.

J decided to cooperate. As he rose from the chair, the figure shoved him back into the chair. "Never mind. Keep your butt in the chair, where I can watch you. I'll turn it on!"

The man pressed the power button with his index finger. Instantaneously, he was thrown some ten feet across the room. As smoke curled around the soles of his shoes and rose from his head, J could smell an odor reminiscent of burnt roast beef.

Acting quickly, he jumped up and grabbed the man's gun. Frantically, he searched for something to tie him up with. When he couldn't find anything, he ran to the phone to call the police, knowing that he only had some thirty minutes before the man regained consciousness. Before he could make the call, he heard footsteps creeping up the hall.

Oh, no, not two of them, J thought. Where the hell was the security guard? Little did J know that the security guard had been given fifty bucks to disappear for several hours while the intruders "surprised an old friend", at least that is what they told the guard.

Turning off the lights again, J stood at the entrance of the door. As the figure crossed the threshold, J tripped him. The man scrambled to his feet and J turned on the light. The intruder turned and lunged at J, missing him by inches. As the figure leaped past him, J swung around quickly and shot him in the leg. At least he thought it was the leg, but closer inspection revealed that he'd shot the stranger in the left side of his butt.

"Oh, man! You've got to get me to a doctor. I'm dying!"

"I am a doctor. That's how I know you're not dying!" J was standing over the second intruder, inspecting the wound. "Tell me why you and your friend over there have come after me?!"

"I'm not talking until you get me a doctor and a lawyer! I'm going to sue you, you son of a biscuit!"

By now J was angry and tired. His only response was to kick the man in his butt and return to his previously interrupted call. Dialing the numbers that had become so painfully familiar, J was able to reach Detective Timothy Dae, the officer working on his brother's disappearance. Within minutes, two squad cars came to pick up the thugs for interrogation. Detective Dae arrived later to personally take J's statement. He assured J that if these men were involved in Geoffrie's disappearance, the police would get to the bottom of it.

Driving home with his nerves worn to a frazzle, J wondered if maybe he should cancel Geoffrie's lecture. He decided not to since he believed that the men who came after him tonight were really after Geoffrie, proving that his plan was working.

As he drove up to Geoffrie's apartment, he saw a shadowy figure standing at the gate. What now? he thought. Drawing closer, he recognized Dr. Duchett, the old chief of surgery who had censored Geoffrie's choice of music in the OR. But what could he want? J thought. He hadn't seen Dr. Duchett since he left St. Barrister's five years ago. Although the old doctor had retired, rumor had it that he'd been asked to leave due to misappropriation of funds.

"Hey. Nice night, isn't it?" Dr. Duchett queried as J exited the rented Corvette.

"Yes, it is, depending on your point of view. What can I do for you, Dr. Duchett?" J's curiosity had reached a new high. How did he know where Geoff lived? After all, they didn't run in the same social circles.

"I thought I might be able to help you locate your brother."

"Look, Dr. D, I'm tired and in no mood to play games. So if you think you know something, spit it out. Otherwise, leave me alone!"

In the few seconds it took J to utter that response, it occurred to him that no one could know Geoffrie was missing unless they were involved in his disappearance. Nothing had been leaked to the press and even Quinn was unaware of Geoffrie's plight. Suddenly, J grabbed Dr. Duchett by the collar and pressed him up against the wrought iron gate. All gentleness had left J and he was filled with rage. "Look, you old goat, you're going to tell me everything you know and then we're going to the police!"

"Not so fast!" Dr. Duchett countered. He was now pressing a silencer to J's chest. In his adrenaline rush, the angry young doctor never saw the older doctor take out a gun. "I'll tell you everything in due time, but we're going to do this my way."

Knowing he was outgunned since he'd left the thug's gun at Geoffrie's lab, J loosened his grip on Dr. Duchett's collar.

The two men walked back to the Corvette and the younger one was forced to drive to a destination, as of yet undetermined. "Where are we going?" J asked.

"You'll know when we get there. Just turn when I tell you and follow my instructions." As the car traveled along, J soon realized they were headed to St. Barrister Hospital. Why on earth would he want to come here? J thought. As they approached the hospital, Dr. Duchett had J drive around back, to the service entrance, where he pulled out a key and opened the door. The two men walked in silence through a hospital tunnel reserved for laundry, janitorial, and food services. J decided not to ask any more questions until they arrived at their destination.

* * * * * * *

When the sound of the dog's footsteps stopped, the hospital door opened and Riff was escorted in by a man in a white leotard and fake leopard coat. This, Dr. Hambrec explained, was Riff's trainer. Geoffrie thought he looked like a reject from a Vegas act.

"In case you're wondering why he's here, you must know it's getting close to lunchtime. We thought you might like to feed him." Dr. Hambrec was smiling quite broadly at this point.

"I don't understand," Geoffrie stammered, almost afraid to open his mouth for fear of the threat of violence, he had been warned about earlier.

"It's okay. We've prepared you with Riff's favorite meal, sirloin steak!"

Geoffrie looked around the room.

"It's in your lap," Dr. Hambrec giggled. "You see, we've placed the best cuts of sirloin over your groin area. Of course, you don't feel anything because you're paralyzed. Although he's not been known to eat human 'giblets,' I guess there's always a first time." Hambrec laughed hysterically, pleased with her own humor.

Geoffrie stared at her in disbelief.

"Cheer up, doc. Whatever happens, you won't feel anything until we reverse the paralysis." Hambrec continued. "Riff will be allowed to eat the steak, and depending on how hungry he is, you may end up missing some vital parts."

Geoffrie was hysterical, unconcerned that he no longer appeared macho.

"But—but I told you I would tell you whatever you want to know!"

"I know what you said, but your eyes tell me you're lying! You're hiding something, and by the time Riff starts lunch, I have a hunch you'll spill your guts!" Hambrec walked away, motioning for Mr. Leopard Coat to bring Riff forward.

Dr. Hambrec, who was no one's doctor, was born Sharon Duchett. She had married her vocal coach and manager, thinking it would advance her career if he was more incentivized to help her. However, he continued to insist that she be perfectly trained and prepared before starting her professional career as a mezzo soprano. Sharon was low on patience and wanted to have her cake and eat it, too. Her dad, Dr. Duchett, did little to dissuade her from the notion that she deserved whatever she wanted and shouldn't let anyone stand in her way. He sent her away to boarding school after her mom died. There was no parenting in her life, at least none that was of any consequence. As a result, Sharon was shallow and self-absorbed. The evil developed after her plans for a professional career fell through. This she blamed on everyone but herself. She had no consciousness of wrong and in general was a sociopath.

* * * * * * *

After traversing the service tunnel, the two doctors reached a sharp turn that led off into what appeared to be a hospital wing, but it was incomplete. On the side of the wall were the words the Dr. Derrix Duchett wing. J was quite astounded. As if to answer his unspoken question, Dr. Duchett cleared his throat almost apologetically and began to explain how construction on the wing had been aborted when he was caught embezzling funds from the hospital. J remembered that Dr. Duchett had retired under a cloud of suspicion and deceit, but had no idea that they had previously begun building a wing in his honor.

Dr. Duchett explained how he had gone into considerable debt trying to support his daughter's lavish lifestyle when her singing career fell through. He explained how Sharon was considered one of the most promising sopranos in the world of opera, but ruined her voice by undergoing an operation on her vocal cords. She felt that this would further intensify her clarity and pitch, virtually ensuring her success. She went to countless doctors, Dr. Duchett continued, and all of them turned her down for various reasons. Finally she black mailed a rather naive ENT specialist into performing the surgery. She threatened to expose their affair to his wife, after she seduced him. As if to add insult to injury, when the operation failed, she sued him. Six months later he committed suicide. She likes to tell everyone her voice was ruined by a botched procedure to remove vocal cord nodules, but it was ruined due to her vanity……his voice trailed off realizing that he had told J more than he needed to know.

J gathered his thoughts and began a barrage of questions. "So, what does this have to do with my brother and me?! Why are we here in this incomplete hospital wing? When can I see my brother? Why—"

"Wait a minute! It'll be clear soon, when I take you to where your brother is! But let me state, for the record, that if I hadn't been involved in that scandal and forced to retire, your brother would never have become chief of surgery. I've always been a better doctor and a better man."

"I don't think so!" J countered.

"Don't forget who has the gun," Dr. Duchett stated, punching it into J's ribs for emphasis.

As they walked down the sterile white corridor, J heard a low-pitched, maniacal laugh that seemed to have its origin in the depths of hell. It was the most sinister, evil laugh he had ever experienced. He couldn't tell if it was male or female.

"That would be Sharon," Dr. Duchett said, answering J's thought.

Just then, Dr. Duchett approached a door ten feet down the hallway. He reached for the knob and opened the door. J entered behind him and saw the most horrific scene he could have ever imagined.

Geoffrie was stretched out on an exam table with his legs spread-eagled. The only thing covering his lower torso was a small apron of sirloin steak, strategically placed.

Standing at his feet was a woman whose eyes were blazing with anger. "Why did you bring him here? I told you everything was under control!" the woman roared.

"That remains to be seen!" Dr. Duchett was obviously angry.

"What is the meaning of this?" He demanded, pointing to Geoffrie's groin. "I thought you were going to be reasonable and level-headed. But, as usual, you've gone to the extreme. Don't you know that if you harm him, he won't be able to help us complete and perfect Super Cell?"

"Look, old man, doctors are a dime a dozen. If we get the secret from these two, any other hack doctor can help us!"

With Duchett and Sharon at odds, J seized his opportunity. He lunged at Dr. Duchett, who had lowered the gun to his side. But before his leap was completed, Duchett re-aimed his gun and shot J in the leg. J dropped to his knees in severe pain. Riff was poised to attack J, as well, when Sharon shouted, "Hold short, Riff!"

Geoffrie, who had fainted earlier after he was told that he was feeding the dog, started to come around. "Hey, what's going on?" No sooner than he had spoken these words than he heard a man groaning in agony. He soon recognized J's voice. "Jonathan! Jonathan! Are you all right?" he shouted.

"I'm okay, man."

"Shut up! Everyone just be quiet!" Sharon shouted.

J clutched his leg as he dragged himself to the nearest chair and tied his sock as a tourniquet around his wounded calf. He had never been shot and found it hard to believe the predicament they were in.

His thoughts were interrupted by Dr. Duchett's impatience. "You two have very few options here, so you better decide quickly if you're going to give us what we want. As a doctor, I do not enjoy anyone's suffering, but I'm prepared to endure your suffering for the good of humanity."

"Your interest in Super Cell is purely for greed and driven by the interest of your daughter's revenge." Geoff was trying to figure out what the next step should be, when Sharon announced the next "entertainment" event.

35

"Guess what? You all are in for a real treat. For the next level of fun, we've collected a few pets of a different kind—"

"Hold off, Sharon. Give them a chance to consider their options before any additional torture takes place."

Sharon angrily left the room, with obvious dissatisfaction.

Redirecting his attention to the doctors Stein, Duchett outlined their options: "You can voluntarily give us the other half of Super Cell, and get richer with us; don't give us Super Cell, and we'll continue to torture you; you die during the process, and we'll hire another doctor/researcher to work with us through completion. The latter will take longer, but either way, Super Cell is ours. Think about it." Duchett left the room.

Geoffrie looked at J and signed to indicate that the room was probably bugged. J never thought sign language would come in handy, but when they were ten years old, their parents had encouraged them to take a course in sign language in order to volunteer at a home for the deaf. With this in mind, they resumed speaking aloud with the intent of disguising their true plans.

J picked up the verbal communication. "Let's consider going into business with this scum; if we refuse, we end up dead and they still get control of Super Cell." During the verbal exchange, the twins continued planning their escape through sign. They decided to fake the delivery of SC by offering up the Datatrex. The second half of Super Cell was somewhere else, still unknown to Geoff. J felt it was best for his brother if he didn't know where it was.

Confirming their suspicion of audio surveillance, Sharon raced into the room. "Okay, Let's do this! I'm kind of disappointed that you're throwing in the towel before the second level of entertainment." She was laughing maniacally. Anticipating further resistance, she had set up a room of starving lab rats. The rats were intentionally infected with deadly viruses previously housed in the research lab to develop vaccines to treat or cure these illnesses. Geoff and J were going to be placed, blindfolded, in this room, clothed in aprons with cheese-laden pockets. The challenge would be to locate the door before being scratched or bitten by hungry vermin. Hambrec just knew that they would give up long before reaching the door. They would be released by pressing a button on the apron, a panic button that indicated their willingness to surrender the location of the second half of Super Cell.

"Okay, docs, how do we get Super Cell Part Two?" Dr. Duchett queried, salivating at the thought of the incredible wealth the technology would generate.

"I'll get it." J volunteered, thinking he would be able to escape anyone they might send with him. He was going to get help! They weren't going to continue to get away with this!

"No. We'll all go! There's no way we're letting either of you out of our sight. Get Riff, you Neanderthals, and let's go," Sharon's hoarse voice called to the two goons that had tied Geoff down.

They untied him and tossed him his clothing.

"Get dressed," Sharon ordered.

"I need to get cleaned up. I can't continue to walk around smelling like raw meat. That rabid dog may try to attack me again." Riff showed his fangs as if to emphasize that possibility.

"If you delay us any longer, that dog will be the least of your problems."

"Okay, Sharon, let him wash up," Duchett prided himself on having raised a daughter who was strong and took charge, but there were times when he felt like he had done too good of a job!

J didn't say anything during this exchange, but his mind was racing toward the next few minutes and the plan that he and Geoff had formulated in sign. They needed to get Sharon or Dr. Duchett to attempt to turn on the Datatrex. This would shock them and create a diversion. But how could they get Duchett and Sharon to do exactly what they wanted, when the villains had all the power and weapons?

"Let the help get the laptop, and we can stay here with our guests." Dr. Duchett had decided that any attempt at relocation might allow Geoffrie and J to escape.

Sharon, agreeing with this, sat down to observe the overall demeanor of the two brothers. She still wondered whether there was any chance she might still get to feed her pets that day.

* * * * * * *

Thirty minutes later, the "help" arrived at Geoff's lab, entering with the key J had supplied. The first Neanderthal located the safe using the map that Geoffrie had drawn. J had placed the Datatrex in the safe the night he was attacked by the two intruders who worked for Hambrec. He hadn't known who they were at the time, but he soon put two and two together. J had been able to put them out of commission, and they were still in the jail's holding cell, one with a gunshot wound to the butt and the other still "half done" from his Datatrex shock.

After opening the safe, Neanderthal One flipped open the lid of the laptop. At that precise moment, he inadvertently touched the power button. The Datatrex quickly accessed his DNA, recognized that this person wasn't Geoff, and delivered an immediate shock. The thug was thrown across the room, with smoke billowing from the soles of his shoes and his hair singed.

Affected by this event, Neanderthal Two quickly called Dr. Hambrec. "What should I do . . . call 911?"

"No, you idiot! They'll have all kinds of questions. Leave him, and bring the laptop!"

"I can't touch that thing. It'll kill me!"

"What happened when Jack was shocked?" Sharon queried.

"I think he tried to turn it on!"

"So don't try to turn it on. Besides, your instructions were to bring it back, not turn it on." Sharon was wondering where she had originally found these roughnecks. They were big on brawn and muscle, but weren't candidates for Mensa.

The remaining neanderthal gingerly picked up the Datatrex, closed the lid, and headed back to the hospital.

Upon his arrival, Sharon demanded to know what had happened.

"All he did was touch this, but then—"

POW!!! The neanderthal sailed across the room. Because it was the second shock in less than thirty minutes, it was twice the voltage of the first shock, as the Datatrex was programmed to do. The man flew across the room with such force that he pushed Hambrec backward and off of her feet. She had been looking over his shoulder when he provoked the Datatrex.

Geoff and J, seizing the opportunity, ran out the door and down the tunnel of the aborted Duchett wing.

"Riff, run!" Hambrec pointed, directing the pit bull to pursue the previously captive doctors.

Because of his wound, J lagged and Riff tackled him from behind. Geoff noticed a housekeeping cart and quickly grabbed a cleaning solution bottle, then sprayed it into the vicious dog's eyes. Riff immediately retreated, whining and pawing at his eyes and face. J caught a strong whiff of ammonia. Thinking fast, he immediately started spraying his own clothing and Geoff's while they resumed running.

"What are you doing, J?"

Just then, bullets started to fly. "I can't keep up," J said. "You keep going!" He stopped and lay on the floor, faint from blood loss. Fortunately, the bullet had gone clean through his leg.

"I can't leave you!"

"Yes, you can. Get help . . . quick!" J's voice was now little more than a whisper due to fatigue and his leg wound.

40

Rushing up on J, Sharon and Duchett dragged him to his feet. He was quickly blindfolded and gagged, with his hands secured behind his back. They pulled him away down the hall, and after what seemed like forever, they stopped and threw him into a room. He heard squealing and realized that he was in a room full of vermin. But, perceiving the strong ammonia odor from the cleaning solution that J had sprayed on his clothing, the animals retreated to the corners of the room, fearing that a hungry predator was present. J tried to figure out how he would escape before the pungent odor faded, allowing the cheese aroma wafting from his pockets to embolden them to attack. Sharon had placed the cheese on J to enhance the rats' interest in him.

Having overheard Dr. Hambrec referencing the rat lab as part of her next level of entertainment, J thought the ammonia might be helpful, although he wasn't quite sure what she had in mind. He recalled an animal program mentioning that when rats smell ammonia, they perceive the possible presence of a predator and retreat!

After ten minutes, Sharon looked through the window of the lab door, enraged that the rats weren't attacking. "We don't have all day. The research lab staff will be here in an hour or so!" Angrily, she jerked open the door of the lab. Dr. Duchett dragged J out and they headed toward the parking lot.

After escaping and exiting the building, Geoff realized that he had no form of transportation. He stumbled out to the highway running north of the main entrance. He knew his only recourse was to try to hitchhike.

Just as he was giving up on anyone traveling that direction at five in the morning, a black pickup truck pulled up in the distance. "Can I give you a lift?" the driver queried.

"I have to get to the nearest police precinct."

The stranger eyed Geoffrie suspiciously, but decided to give him a ride.

As Geoffrie closed the door, the stranger got a strong whiff of the ammonia that J had sprayed on him. Geoffrie could smell it as well, in the closed vehicle. He suspected that the man may have thought he peed on himself, but felt it was best to not try to offer any explanation.

As the stranger pulled up to the third precinct (the closest according to the GPS), he was happy to get rid of the smelly man who seemed he might be dangerous. He was more than ready to drop him off directly into the hands of law enforcement.

Approaching the night clerk's desk, Geoffrie tried to straighten his disheveled clothing. "Good evening, officer. I need to reach Detective Dae immediately. He works in the fifth precinct." He gave a general explanation for his appearance, but few details.

"I'll try to contact him . . . but you say that you've been in the hands of kidnappers for several days?" The clerk was very skeptical. He thought Geoffrie may be delusional since he had nothing to corroborate his story or verify his identity. However, there was something about him that was believable. In the meantime, he put Geoffrie in a cell just in case his intuition was wrong and this man turned out to be dangerous after all.

Thirty minutes later, Detective Dae arrived at the station. Geoffrie rapidly detailed the events of the previous forty-eight hours, which seemed more like a week.

"Okay, let's get back to the hospital to rescue your brother!" the detective decided.

Arriving back at the hospital, Geoff took the detective to the abandoned Duchett wing. The corridor was completely dark now.

"Honestly, I don't know where to start." Geoff looked around, somewhat frustrated.

"We can track him!" Detective Dae responded.

"You got a bloodhound in your pocket, detective?"

"No, I have something better." The detective pulled out a small, smooth, rectangular black object with a vented surface. "Now all we need is something of your brother's."

"I don't have anything . . ." Geoff's voice trailed off as he put his hands in his pockets and pulled out the sock that J had used as a tourniquet. He handed it to Dae.

Dae pulled away from the blood-soaked sock and handed the device to Geoffrie. "All you have to do is push the red button and hold it close to the sock. It will sense the odor and store it in memory. Once it detects the same odor in the surrounding air, it will beep. The stronger the signal, the louder the beep."

As the device beeped, Geoffrie and Dae followed the beeping down the corridor in the direction of the brothers' earlier attempted escape. With this display, Geoffrie was convinced the device actually worked. It continued to beep until it led them to the rat lab. Looking in the window, Dae could see that J was no longer there. Only squealing rats were in the room. Geoff shuddered at the thought that J had been tortured or tested by the vicious vermin. He could only pray that his brother wasn't bitten by any of the inhabitants of the lab since he knew they were infected with incurable diseases.

As the sensor beeped louder, leading them to the parking lot, Geoffrie and the detective heard voices.

"Well where do *you* think we should take him?" Sharon turned and snarled at Duchett, angry that nothing was working out as planned.

"I know exactly where we'll take him. Let me drive." Duchett jumped into the driver's side of the van.

Dae eased into the lot, gun drawn. Working his way around various vehicles, he tried to sneak up on the two assailants. Just then, the sensor that Dae thought he had turned off beeped loudly and incessantly.

"What's that noise? Get in!" Sharon motioned to Duchett, who pushed J inside the van. J was bound, gagged, and blindfolded, so he was unaware of what was going on until he heard his brother yell.

"Hey, J! Man, are you okay?"

Unable to answer, J stumbled as he was pushed into the van.

"Let's go!" Sharon yelled, and they sped off in the van.

Detective Dae and Geoffrie rushed to the unmarked police car, they had arrived in.

Close in pursuit, Dae shoved an object at Geoff that appeared to be a gun. "Here. Use this!"

"My brother's in that van! I'm not going to shoot recklessly."

"It's not a gun! It's a GPS sensor."

With that info, Geoffrie took aim and shot a gelatinous pellet that hit its target with a dull thud.

"Now we can hang back and let them think they lost us at some point. We'll continue to track them from a distance."

Five minutes later and several blocks behind, Geoffrie started to see familiar sights. "Hey, I know this hood." He looked out the window and noticed a deli that he had been to several times. Just then the car slowed down. "Why are you creeping along?"

"We're arriving at the destination of the van. I want to park around the rear so I can call for backup while we sneak in!"

As they turned onto the street where the van had gone just minutes earlier, Geoffrie realized they were on the street where Quinn lived.

As they got closer, he saw Sharon at Quinn's front door, having a heated conversation with her. Geoffrie was totally confused. His mind was rushing. Why were they at her home, and how did she know these kidnappers? He couldn't hear what was being said, but Quinn was angry and appeared to know Sharon.

Sharon returned to the van parked behind the house and motioned to Duchett to get J out. Stumbling along as Duchett pushed him toward the house, J wondered where and why he was being moved.

Stumbling up several steps, he heard a door open and smelled a familiar scent, but couldn't pinpoint where he'd encountered it before.

Just then, an effervescent voice infused with anger wanted to know, "Why did you bring him here?"

J became weak in the knees as he recognized Quinn's voice. He didn't know if it was from the loss of blood or the emotional betrayal he felt in that instant.

Pushing their way inside, Sharon and Duchett advised Quinn that they had been unable to secure Super Cell and that the other brother had escaped. "Well, we have to get rid of this one, because he knows you—"

"And you," J interjected, wanting to confront Quinn.

Not addressing J, she turned to the two criminals. "Leave! I'll take care of him and catch up with you later."

"How?" Sharon demanded. "We don't need any loose ends."

"Never you mind; you and your idiot dad have already botched things!"

46

"I'm staying!" Sharon was staunchly determined to witness J's demise. Without any warning, Quinn suddenly landed an uppercut to J's chin, knocking him out of the chair. She then grabbed a dagger out of her belt and stabbed his chest with several quick movements. He was barely conscious, but noticed that with the blows he didn't feel the tearing sensation he expected from a knife. He did feel warm fluid on his chest.

Sharon rushed over. "That's not good enough. Let me slit his throat!"

"No! I'm not going to be stuck here cleaning up all the blood. It will be enough to get rid of the body."

Suddenly they heard loud crashing sounds at the front and back doors. Dae and SWAT entered both simultaneously. Seeing J wounded and bleeding, Dae told the backup officer to call 911 and turned to assess J's ABCs. Pulse was present but rapid. He tore off J's shirt to examine the wound. "Hey, his skin is intact. There's no wound!"

Snatching the dagger out of Quinn's hand and throwing it to the floor, Detective Dae noticed that it was amazingly light.

The SWAT leader picked up the knife. "Hey, this thing isn't real! This is one of those theatrical jobbies."

"Doesn't matter. She's under arrest!" Dae grabbed Quinn and handcuffed her. Reciting the Miranda rights, he pushed her toward the door. She remained stoically silent. Geoffrie, finally unrestrained, rushed in to find J on the floor, "bleeding". Rushing toward Quinn with uncontrollable anger, he lunged at her, not knowing what he would do, only knowing that he needed to inflict pain. What he thought was blood was actually red dye from the handle of the faux dagger that was released, when Quinn applied pressure to the handle.

Hurt by the pain in Geoffrie's eyes, Quinn could only say, "Geoff, there's a reason for all of this. Trust me." By then the paramedics had arrived and declared that J was stable. The only blood loss was from the gunshot wound to his leg, but it was still enough to make him weak.

Geoffrie jumped into the ambulance just as it was pulling away. The paramedics did a double take, realizing that the patient and their passenger were identical. As the paramedics started an IV, J and Geoffrie attempted to understand how Quinn was involved in the events of the past few days. Nothing was making sense, so Geoff decided to go to the police station after J was checked out at the hospital.

Stopping at the desk, he asked to speak with Detective Dae. He was escorted to the detective's desk, at the back of the precinct.

"Hey, Dr. Stein. How's your brother?"

"He's going to be fine . . . but he's upset about Quinn. What's going to happen to her?"

"Oh, she's been gone for an hour or so."

"What do you mean, she's gone?!"

"She's a federal agent, and when she met you and your brother, she was building a case against Duchett and his daughter. When she first started to explain, I didn't believe her, but we contacted the federal agency and it checked out."

"Well, I need to speak with her. She still has some explaining to do!" Detective Dae wished him luck.

Geoffrie and Quinn were still engaged, but this changed everything. Arriving at Quinn's house, he saw her assessing the damage where SWAT had broken down the door.

Somewhat relieved to see Geoff, Quinn managed a half smile, wondering if he was still angry, and if so, just how angry. But she didn't wait for him to say anything. "When I met J at that medical conference a year ago, I was working on a case involving Hambrec and Duchett. The federal agency suspected them of counterfeiting prescription drugs. I was assigned the task of gathering evidence to support our suspicion. While surveilling them, I discovered that they were gathering intel on you and J. In order to determine their interest in you, I needed to get closer to you and your brother. Once I actually met J at the conference, and saw him several times that week, I realized that I was starting to get too involved. In order to distance myself and still remain objective, I chose to focus my attention on you."

"So, can you honestly, tell me that you could care for J and don't have any feelings for me? We're identical!"

"Only in looks!"

"What was that uppercut about, and the stabbing?" It was Geoffrie's turn to interrupt.

"First off, I didn't stab J. I had to fake that attack in order to save his life. Hambrec wanted to kill him, and I had to act fast to make her think I was going to kill him first. She and her dad, Dr. Duchett, were desperate after they realized they weren't going to get Super Cell from you or J. So now the case is closed. Hambrec and Duchett are in federal agency custody for drug counterfeiting and kidnapping."

"So, all's well that ends well?" Geoff asked, still amazed that Quinn had never been interested in him.

"No. I have to know—how's J doing?"

"He'll be released from the hospital tomorrow. He'll want to know what happened today and why," Geoff responded.

"You can explain it to him. Please, tell him I am so sorry. I wish things had turned out differently."

"No, you need to speak to him directly. You've advised me that our engagement wasn't real and you had, or have, feelings for him. I don't know which is the case. So whatever's going on, he needs to hear it straight from you." Geoffrie was determined not to let Quinn off that easily. He also knew that J had never gotten over him "stealing" Quinn's affection and needed closure. "Come to Chez Charrise at 7:00 p.m. tomorrow. You can apologize in person and explain the past two to three days and your role as a federal agent."

"I don't believe he'll want to see me!"

"That may be true, but we'll see tomorrow. Just be there!"

As Geoffrie left, Quinn couldn't believe how alike, but so utterly different, Geoff and J were. As she pondered this paradox, she sat down at her Steinway to tickle the ivories and try to relax after one of the most trying days she'd had in a while. This had also been one of her most difficult cases—not so much the planning and execution, but the emotional toll.

Usually she made it a point not to become emotionally attached to case subjects. That made it easy to detach and disappear once the case was completed. But now, to make matters worse, she was going to have to meet with a case subject and explain her actions. This wasn't usual. Once Geoff and J were told she was a federal agent, that should have been it. She should have walked away and never laid eyes on them again! Now Geoff felt that she owed J an explanation and, because she had developed feelings for J, she thought she owed him one, too. She was going to have to hang around and be interrogated. Well, she certainly hadn't bargained for that!

After all, she had never lied to either one of them. She was everything she said she was: a trained but non-practicing MD who chose to teach instead. What she didn't mention was that she was recruited to the federal agency soon after she completed medical school and residency. Because of her youthful appearance, they had approached her to work undercover on college and high school campuses as a teacher and sometimes a student. They especially chose her to investigate and target Hambrec and Duchett for counterfeiting prescription meds, because of her medical background. Geoff and J just happened to be a subplot. Quinn, not looking forward to the next day, decided that it was what it was, and she was going to have to face the music. It just wasn't the kind she was used to.

She continued to play her piano, which was now somewhat of an antique. The old Steinway was bought brand-new by her dad some thirty-plus years ago, when she first started taking lessons. She had natural talent and was classically trained. After a few junior competitions and concerts, she decided it wasn't the career of her choice, but she was happy that it was a great diversion in times such as these.

The next day, Geoff picked J up at the hospital. "Hey, old man, how you feelin'?"

"You're the old man, even if it's just by a few minutes."

J managed a weak smile, still tired from the last few days and the gunshot wound that still hurt despite the meds. "Let's just get home. Call the hospital and let them know I'll be taking some time off."

"Don't worry, I've taken care of that. I didn't have to go into a lot of detail." Geoffrie continued. "Since the arrest of Hambrec and Duchett, the story has been all over the news. You also need to bring me up to speed on this Super Cell thing you've been working on. After all, it almost got us killed and has been the cause of all this havoc."

"Yes, in due time. Right now I just want to rest."

"Cool. I'll come by later and we'll go to Chez Charrise for dinner."

J felt like staying in the rest of the day, but didn't want to cook, so he reluctantly agreed.

That night, when they arrived at Chez Charrise, Geoff and J sat at their favorite table. Just as they were ordering, J looked up to see Quinn approaching the table.

Geoffrie knew before he looked up from the menu that Quinn had arrived. J's tone became icy and his shoulders and posture stiffened up. Geoffrie jumped up and pulled out a chair for Quinn.

"Thank you." She smiled at the two brothers. The effervescence of her voice was still familiar to J, but he felt as if he didn't know this Quinn, the one who had betrayed his trust, physically assaulted him, and was now smiling as if nothing had transpired in the past few days.

Quinn started slowly, assessing J's mood. "I know you must be angry and confused, J." She went on to explain the evolution of their relationship and how it was initially based on a federal agency investigation. However, she quickly reassured him that as they'd spent time together at the conference, she'd begun to care for him and had to switch her attention to Geoffrie in order to remain objective.

J began to soften his demeanor as Quinn explained the events of the recent days from her perspective. "So, when I was pretending to be Geoff, you knew it was me?" By now, J was laughing uncontrollably, recalling his efforts to maintain his cover as his world-renowned brother. Geoffrie was outgoing, aggressive, and very well liked. J was agreeable but quiet and introspective, qualities that Quinn found attractive and endearing. As they continued to talk, it became obvious to Geoffrie that he was the third wheel.

He quietly excused himself and paid the bill. He knew this was where he had come in a year before, when he'd stolen J's date. Now it was time for him to repay the favor and leave. He knew Quinn would make sure his brother made it home safely.

CHICAGO

ADVENTURE

GREED

KIDNAPPING

SIBLING RIVALRY

Bithia's Vacay

CHICAGO

ADVENTURE

GREED

KIDNAPPING

SIBLING RIVALRY

Bithia's Vacay

I, Bithia Blake, being of sound mind and body, do hereby declare that I will go postal if I do not get a vacation soon. I have been working nonstop except on weekends, and the stress is never-ending. Thia knew that these thoughts would appear desperate to anyone who was not in her situation, but she didn't care. Just being able to acknowledge the fact that she was at her breaking point allowed her to not feel guilty about taking one week off, even in the middle of what must have been the busiest work period she had experienced in years.

Psychiatry was already an untenable occupation based on bearing the weight of other people's mental health. She had always tried not to take her work home, but with the types of cases she was seeing lately, it was becoming more difficult. Just the other day, she'd had to counsel a whole family that was being impacted by the bipolar illness of a son. The mother was unable to attend to the needs of her other two kids because her son demanded all her attention and wouldn't take his prescribed meds. She, the mom, was giving him the meds; but he was holding them in his mouth and spitting them out later. This was evidenced by a small stash of soggy pills hidden away in a corner drawer of the son's dresser. She wasn't intentionally snooping; she'd found them one day as she was putting away his laundry. She and her husband wondered why their son wasn't getting better. They decided that Dr. Blake didn't know what she was doing and wasn't giving him the right medication. This had come out at an earlier "emergency" meeting, during which the mother demanded the right to bring her son in for a same-day appointment. Bithia agreed to change his medications, but of course there was no improvement, and the boy's mother had found out why. However, she hadn't discovered the pills before calling the office and threatening to report Dr. Blake to the AMA based on what she considered incompetence.

This and the everyday strain of managing office staff, the daily expenses of the practice, and family matters were more than the thirty-three-year-old doctor had bargained for when she first decided that she wanted to be a doctor. She had also expected to have her own family by now, but the daily pressures of starting and maintaining a practice made that difficult. However, as of today, she was going to start looking after Thia (the name friends called her for short). She had booked her plane ticket and made hotel reservations over a month before, heading to Miami.

So, after completing her packing the day before, she had gone to bed, finally anticipating being able to eat and sleep well for at least a week. She scheduled an Uber and gave herself four hours to get to the airport, allowing for traffic mishaps or security delays. She wanted this to be a stress-free vacation, and she didn't want to start it with any problems before she actually arrived.

Getting to O'Hare with ample time, she checked in and headed toward security. Placing her laptop in one bin and her carry-on and shoes in another, she confidently went through the imaging machine. She had remembered not to wear anything metallic, to empty her pockets of change and keys, and to confine her liquids to less than six ounces. Yes, this was going to go seamlessly if she had anything to say about it.

After passing through security, she picked up her shoes and carry-on luggage. The first bin, the one that had held her laptop, was empty! Startled and angry, she whirled around and quickly surveyed the conveyor belt again. Out of the corner of her eye, she saw her computer in the wheelchair of the passenger who had passed through security in front of her. The elderly lady was being helped by her son. Swiftly, Thia lunged forward and grabbed the laptop.

The son looked startled, but then quickly apologized. "I'm so sorry; my mom told me that was one of her bags!" Thia knew that this was a lie from the pit; the son and mom were traveling together, so he knew which items they had placed on the belt, and her laptop wasn't one of them. Not bothering to convict the son verbally, she walked away, having averted her first disaster. Her laptop was secured with three layers of protection as well as two types of security software, but she knew that nothing was infallible. She hoped she wouldn't need the computer for work, but she wanted to be able to check her email and contact family while away. Most people used smartphones, but Thia couldn't bear to give up her laptop and still enjoyed the luxury of the "big screen." However, with this most recent near disaster, she was seriously starting to rethink the benefits of a more portable device.

Walking to the gate, she wondered if she had time to stop and pick up a small bag of popcorn, something she could munch on during the flight. She was flying first class, but didn't always find the food enjoyable. The leg room was always great and allowed her to sleep comfortably without someone's elbow in her side or knees in her back.

Opting to skip the popcorn, she found the gate and settled in comfortably. With more than an hour before boarding, she took out a book to read. Not more than twenty or thirty minutes later, she awakened. She hadn't realized she was tired enough to doze off. That wasn't part of the plan; she would rest once she arrived at her destination. Looking around, she confirmed that her carry-on and laptop were still secure in the chair beside her.

Determined not to fall asleep again, Thia went to the nearest coffee kiosk to get energized. She made sure to take her things so as not to lose sight of them. Having paid for her coffee, she returned to the gate just in time to board. When she arrived in Miami, Thia arranged Uber transport to a downtown hotel.

At the front desk, all was moving smoothly until she heard, "Okay, Dr. Blake, we just need an ID and major credit card for incidentals."

Reaching for her wallet in her back pocket, Thia was appalled to realize that the familiar bulge was missing. Although she never kept her credentials or credit card in her purse, she frantically searched it anyway. Fortunately, she'd kept her passport separate in her opposite jean pocket. "Here's my passport, but I can't find my wallet."

"Let me check with the manager to see what we can do." Now regarding her with a certain level of suspision, the clerk summoned the senior manager.

"Hi, Dr. Blake," the manager greeted her. "What seems to be the problem, John?" He turned to the junior staff.

After explaining Dr. Blake's lack of credit cards, John looked to the manager for the final decision.

"Since you've stayed here multiple times, we will allow you forty-eight hours to come up with a means of payment, after which time you'll have to make alternate arrangements."

Dr. Blake breathed a sigh of partial relief, knowing that she still needed to locate the number for her security credit card service and place a hold on the two credit cards she'd brought with her. She stepped into the elevator, her mind in a whirlwind. The last time she could recall having her wallet was when she paid for her coffee. Had she left it on the counter, or did someone lift it from her pocket after she secured her purchase? Usually she was quite clear on purchase details, but lately she had been so tired, details that were usually taken for granted weren't being automatically recorded in her subconscious.

Arriving in the luxurious room, she pulled up her directory on her flip phone. She speed-dialed her credit card service and detailed her situation. The representative confirmed that there was no new activity on her cards. This, they stated, was unusual since stolen cards are usually used right away to attempt to maximize charges before the owner notices the loss. Thia was able to obtain details on another card, one she'd left at home. Providing this to the hotel manager, she secured her room for the remainder of her stay. Soon after her arrangements were made, her cell phone rang, showing a call from an "unknown private caller." Without thinking, she picked up.

"Hi," the voice said, sounding friendly enough. "I've found your wallet. If you can meet me in thirty minutes, I'll return it to you. You must be worried sick! Meet me outside of your hotel lobby, at 3:30pm." Before Dr. Blake could query him about how and where her wallet had been found, the phone went dead.

Skeptical but wanting to get her cards and driver's license returned, she prepared herself to meet with the stranger. Earlier than the thirty minutes designated, Thia waited anxiously in front of the hotel. At precisely 3:30 p.m., a black Benz with tinted windows rolled up. The door opened. Before Thia could react, she was shoved in and blindfolded. A gruff, mechanically altered voice stated, "You'll get your cards and license back, but you'll help us first! We have a suitcase that you're going to get through airport security for us."

"I'm no smuggler. What can I do that you can't?"

"You'll bring a suitcase of contraband into Chicago. Normally, drugs can be sniffed out, but we've solved that problem, so they shouldn't be detectable by drug-sniffing dogs. If you get through security, someone will meet you in baggage claim. They'll take the suitcase and hand over your things. If you don't make it through, the license and credit cards will be the least of your worries."

"What makes you think I can't replace those items? After all, the cards have been canceled."

"If you go to the authorities, we'll plant your documents at a crime scene to implicate you as the perpetrator. You won't know the crime or circumstances until the authorities track you down and arrest you."

"I've reported those cards stolen."

"Yeah, but how likely are they to believe that without any unauthorized charges? But don't worry; we also took the liberty of obtaining DNA from your toothbrush while you were asleep at the airport."

Thia remembered thinking that the contents of her carry-on bag looked altered, but since nothing was missing, she didn't think too much of it. Now she knew it had been tampered with. But why did they choose her?

What she didn't know was that this experiment had been in the works for a while. She was merely a victim of opportunity, targeted when she was noted to be a woman traveling alone, who was tired and whose state of mind appeared clouded.

"Before you leave, the suitcase will be delivered to your room. The hotel staff will be advised that this is lost luggage being returned to you. Do you understand? Vacation as you normally would. If it appears that you're trying to contact the authorities, remember, you'll be framed for a crime. Believe you me, it will be a serious one."

The Benz pulled up about a block from her hotel and Thia was shoved out as it slowed down. Landing on her palms, she quickly sat up, ripped the blindfold off, and saw the hotel in the distance. She made her way back to the hotel in a daze, not really remembering how she arrived.

She knew she'd walked, but didn't remember putting one foot in front of the other. She was terrified and unsure of what to do next. Hungry, but almost too scared to go anywhere, she decided the best option was to order room service and stay close to the hotel, at least until she decided on the next step.

The kidnappers hadn't told her when the contraband suitcase would arrive, so she was determined to make sure she was there to accept it personally. She didn't dare risk it being delivered to the wrong room since her safety and well-being depended on getting it through airport security.

Back in her room, she quickly ordered shrimp primavera, salad, and a bottle of wine from room service. The food came quickly enough, but Thia was more afraid than hungry. Recounting everything that had happened that morning, she still couldn't figure out how a perfectly planned vacation had gone so wrong.

She turned on the TV and found a game show to keep her mind occupied until the dreaded suitcase arrived. Although she hadn't been told the suitcase would arrive today, something about the urgency of the perpetrators seem to imply a same-day delivery.

About an hour later, there was an incessant knock at the door. Thia awakened from a much-deserved deep sleep. "Hold on, I'm coming!" Stumbling to the door, Thia looked through the peephole. The waiting bellboy appeared somewhat irritated. Thia could only imagine how long he had waited since she'd been fast asleep. When she opened the door, he immediately confirmed that she was Bithia Blake and handed her a plain brown suitcase after she signed the receipt.

Treating the suitcase like an unexploded grenade, she gently placed it on the hotel desk. Vowing not to open it, she backed away, thinking this might be the best way to keep her curiosity from getting the best of her. After all, curiosity killed the cat, if you believe the adage.

By 5:00 p.m., Thia was eyeing the suitcase, trying to determine if looking inside would violate any unspoken agreement with the thugs. Finally she decided that since she was going to be transporting an illegal substance, she deserved to know exactly what it was.

Springing the latch, she braced herself and leaned backward in case of any explosion. Strangely enough, nothing happened. Inside, there were skirts, slacks, and long-sleeved shirts with lots of buttons (button-down collars, buttoned pockets, and double-button cuffs). Why so many buttons? she thought. But more importantly, no drugs! Was this some kind of cruel joke?

Just then the phone rang, causing her to jump. She felt guilty, but justified her right to open the suitcase because she was taking the risk of transporting it. Picking up the phone, she heard the electronically altered voice on the other end demand, "Did it arrive?"

"Yes," Bithia responded. Since there were only clothes inside, she made a point of describing the suitcase to make sure she had the correct luggage.

"That's it," the voice advised her. Bithia wanted to mention the fact that there were no drugs in the suitcase, but was afraid that maybe she wasn't supposed to have opened it. But what if she got to Chicago and they thought she took the drugs? At the very thought, Bithia nearly passed out.

In the last few hours, she had experienced more stress than she had undergone in the past few weeks at work. Maybe she should have tried vacationing at home—yes, a good old-fashioned "staycay."

Coming back to reality, she realized that she had promised to meet with a friend from med school while in town. They were to hang out for at least two days; the remaining five days, she planned to chill at the oceanfront hotel and catch up on her reading. There were at least three books that she had been trying to complete for months. However, she was so rattled, she couldn't begin to pick up a book. She needed to figure out what to do with the contraband suitcase. Thia decided to call Kae to see about getting together for a few drinks and some sightseeing. Kae was born and raised in Tampa, and was well versed on things to do in the area.

Kae was excited to hear from her. "Hey, T! Sup? I wasn't sure if you were still coming!"

"Yeah, girl, I'm here! Just tired." Thia knew she needed to be able to confide in someone, but she wasn't ready to discuss the events of the past twenty-four hours. Plus she wasn't sure how safe it would be to tell anyone about the suitcase and the riffraff that had gotten her involved in their criminal scheme.

"Thia, why don't I swing by, and we'll go to dinner and get drinks, and maybe hit a comedy club?"

"I'm game, for now." Thia new that she might need to beg off before the end of the evening, but she was willing to at least start the evening. Just then she remembered the room service meal. She quickly stuffed the plates into the mini-fridge, thinking they might come in handy for a late-night snack. It was just 5:30 p.m., but it felt like this day had been going on forever.

At six thirty, Kae arrived dressed in designer gear, business casual with comfortable shoes. Not one to put fashion over comfort, Thia noted that her friend always looked dope, even without trying. This was a good thing since Kae was somewhat clumsy and tended to upend, topple, and spill things with minimal yet unintentional effort.

Thia, after taking a long shower, was waiting for Kae when she arrived. Not making much of an effort, Thia put on jeans, a designer T-shirt, and gym shoes, and called it a fashion day.

Reliving the events of the day, Thia nearly jumped out of her skin when there was a loud banging at the door and the sound of New Year's Eve noisemakers. Snatching open the door, she was met with a burst of confetti thrown with wild abandon by Kae, who was smiling broadly. Seeing Kae, Thia couldn't believe it had been ten years since they had last seen each other. They'd kept in touch by phone and letter, but other than on Skype, had not been face-to-face in absolute years. It was just recently that Kae had moved back to Florida, making a reunion easy. Kae looked good; this was despite two divorces and a bankruptcy. Kae could make the money, but she couldn't keep it long enough to manage it. This fact was supported by her arrival in a red Maserati with a black interior, which she proudly pointed out from Thia's hotel room window.

After admiring Kae's latest indulgence, Thia grabbed her purse and they headed to the lobby.

"Where we goin', girl?" Thia queried, trying to suppress her worry.

"You'll see!" Kae responded. They jumped into the flashy car. Kae engaged the ignition and applied more pressure to the gas than Thia would have liked. They sped away in a cloud of smoke and burnt rubber. So much for peace, serenity, and calmness, Thia mused.

Thirty minutes later, they arrived at a nondescript building covered in black marble. The valet was more than happy to take the reins of the latest-model Maserati that had been purchased less than a month before. The maître d' acknowledged Kae with a nod and escorted them to a back room labeled VVIP. Thia was familiar with VIP rooms, but wondered what additional comforts an extra V could add to such an experience. Suddenly she felt extremely underdressed. As they sat at a glass table with crystal glasses and linen napkins, the waiter informed them of the specials and introduced them to their manicurist and pedicurist for the evening. That's right, the extra V was for the luxury of having your hands and feet massaged and cared for while your own personal server fed you your meal! To top it off, Kae (or Dr. Scott, as she was known to the staff), didn't need an appointment since she was a platinum member.

From the appetizers all the way through to dessert, Thia felt as if she had left planet Earth and was in a different galaxy, where hardworking, overstressed women were truly appreciated. However, at the end of the experience, she reentered the Milky Way, when the extravagant bill arrived bringing her back to reality. It included a gratuity for a total of $2,200. Taking out her elite platinum card, she was prepared to share the bill with Kae. Even though she hadn't anticipated this level of expense, it had taken her mind far away from her concerns. She was also concerned that Kae might be overextending herself and might be headed for financial trouble, like before, when she'd had to declare bankruptcy. Not wanting to appear judgmental, she chose her words carefully as she tried to broch the subject.

"Kae, this was great! How often do you come here?" That was subtle, Thia thought.

"As often, as I can!" Kae responded, feeling that she had truly impressed her friend.

"How often might that be?" Thia tried to conceal the alarm she felt.

Kae responded, now realizing that the questions stemmed more from being concerned than impressed. "Don't worry." She paused. "Maybe two to three times a year. Just special occasions! You're a special occasion, so you can put your card away!"

Thia smiled, only slightly relieved, still thinking that more than two times a year for this experience was overdoing it!

They headed back to the hotel just past 10:00 p.m., and Thia invited Kae to spend the night in her suite since there was a sleeper sofa in the living room.

After bringing in linen from the suite closet for Kae to make up the sofa sleeper, Thia retired for the night.

Kae decided, rather than sleep in her underwear, she would borrow one of Thia's shirts that she could rinse out in the morning. Not wanting to disturb Thia, she went directly to one of her suitcases on the side cocktail table. Kae opened a brown, otherwise nondescript suitcase that she felt was a bit out of character for Thia, but who was she to judge? Everyone couldn't be as fashion forward as herself. After choosing a white long-sleeved shirt, she made herself comfortable and turned on the flat screen. Thirty minutes into a late-night talk show, Kae was hungry again. She quickly found the shrimp primavera and made short work of it. In her haste to satiate her hunger, she spilled sauce on the sleeve. Not to worry—she would wash it out and dry it before Thia awakened the next morning.

In the bathroom, Kae placed the shirt in the sink, ran cold water in the basin, and generously poured some hotel shampoo over the stain. She decided to let it soak overnight.

Thia awakened early, not having slept well the night before. Walking into the sitting area, she saw Kae fast asleep. Thia decided to order room service, and they could enjoy breakfast before Kae drove back home.

As Thia walked past the brown suitcase, it appeared to have been moved, but she thought she was just being paranoid since the latch was still fastened. She walked into the bathroom, casually glancing at the white long-sleeved shirt that Kae had borrowed. She almost screamed as she recognized the shirt from the contraband suitcase. Those triple-buttoned cuffs were the first thing she had noted about the shirts. She'd wondered why they had so many buttons and looked so '70s. But more importantly, as she lifted the shirt up now, she could see that the buttons were gone! What the heck? Thia's mind was in a total panic. First there was no contraband in a suitcase that was supposed to be smuggled into Chicago for that very reason. Now there were buttons missing from one of the shirts. Why would Kae soak the shirt?

As if awakening on cue, Kae called from the other room, "Hey, girl, you up? By the way, I borrowed one of your shirts to sleep in, and I spilled food on it. But don't worry, it's soaking in the bathroom."

Thia exclaimed, "Why did you do that?"

"I didn't think you would mind. The shirt was horribly out of style anyway, and not even your size!" Kae was defensive at this point. "It was just a shirt."

"Yeah, right! Where are the buttons?"

"What do you mean, where are the buttons? Are you accusing me of stealing buttons off of a cheap shirt?! Why are you so bent out of shape about a cheap, out-of-style rag?"

In that minute, Thia had an aha moment. The buttons were gone because they were the contraband that was now dissolved in the shampoo, in the bathroom sink. Thia had to decide if she should tell Kae about the thugs and the contraband, but confiding in her would endanger her well-being as well. There were remaining buttons on the other clothes that, more than likely, were also made of drugs. In that instant, Thia decided to keep Kae in the dark. To tell her would only place her in danger.

"You're right . . . don't worry about the shirt. I have plenty of clothes. Let's go to breakfast!"

Kae wasn't ready to let it go. She still had questions. "Why isn't that shirt your size? It's clearly too large . . . and why doesn't that suitcase match your other luggage? You're obviously hiding something, and I want to know what it is."

"Kae, I can't answer all of your questions right now. But once I've cleared everything up, I'll tell you. Can we just go to breakfast for now?" Thia was already devising a plan, or at least the beginning of one. First, she was going to need to replace those buttons. She would take a picture of the buttons on the clothing in the mysterious suitcase and try to match them at a local department store. Before that could happen, she needed to get Kae out of her hair and literally out of the contraband suitcase.

"Well, let me have a closer look at the suitcase." As Kae walked toward the case, Thia lunged past her and grabbed it. Kae reached and pulled on the handle. The case popped open and the clothing tumbled out. Angrily, Thia grabbed the clothing and started folding it back up and placing it in the suitcase.

"I'm sorry, Thia!" Kae reached for a shirt to fold. As she did, she furtively pulled one of the buttons off and hid it. Thia was quiet as she continued replacing the clothing.

"Kae, I'm trying to keep you out of this, but you just keep interfering. Why won't you let it go?"

Kae knew that Thia needed help; she just didn't know how much help, and how serious the matter was. So she decided to agree verbally to leave the matter alone. In her heart, Kae was determined to help.

"Okay, Thia, you win. Let's go to breakfast. But if you change your mind, let me know."

They went to a local chicken and waffle house in Kae's Maserati. Thia felt as if they were being followed, but couldn't be sure. After all, anyone in a $150,000 plus car was bound to get a certain amount of attention. She didn't mention this to Kae because she knew the questions would resume. Her friend was relentless when she was determined to get to the bottom of any situation. It wasn't a bad trait, just annoying at times—and this was one of those times.

Finishing up breakfast, Thia paid the bill and the two friends parted ways. Just then, Thia noticed a woman in a dark jacket and slacks hovering in the background. She hadn't seen her before, but then she hadn't seen her abductors when she'd been thrown in the car the previous day, either. Being blindfolded, the only thing she could recall were voices, which had all been male. Well, maybe I'm just being paranoid, she thought. Keep it simple. Just get back to the hotel and find a way to replace the buttons. After calling an Uber, she went to a local store recommended by the concierge. She found buttons close enough to pass for the originals, then returned to the hotel and used the complimentary sewing kit to attach them.

In the meantime, Kae called a close friend who was a detective at a nearby precinct.

"Hi, Detective Geffer. I need a favor. Can I get you to analyze a clothing article for me? A button?"

"Since it's not involving a police case, I would need to do it carefully, but I can get it done. But why do you want to analyze a button?"

"That's just it—I don't think it's just a button. I've seen these buttons dissolve in water!"

"Maybe they're just made of cheap materials. Is there anything else about these buttons that warrant the use of police resources?"

"Well, they were in a mysterious suitcase full of clothing that my friend has. But the clothes don't fit her and she doesn't want anyone else to handle them. She won't explain to me why she has these clothes, and she's just acting strange."

"That doesn't prove anything, but I'll help you out. Bring the button to the precinct and meet me at the front desk."

Thirty minutes later, Kae arrived with a brown envelope that was clasped and sealed. Detective George Geffer was paged to the front desk, and he took the envelope, reassuring Kae that he would get back to her as soon as he had any information.

Thia, resting in the hotel, felt more tired than when she started her vacation. By now it was 5:00 p.m. Nothing she tried calmed her fears. She tossed and turned, as she tried to sleep. The next morning she awakened to the ringing of her cell phone. Looking at the screen, she saw it was Kae. Wow, this woman gets up early, Thia thought. Then, looking at the time, she saw it was 8:00 a.m.

"Where have you been?" Kae asked. "I've been trying to reach you for hours!"

"Really, Kae? It's just 8:00 a.m., and I am on vacation, after all."

"Well, you need to know—we in trouble!"

"First off, *we* are not in trouble. *I* am in trouble." Thia made it a point to correct Kae's lapse into less than grammatically correct English, which happened whenever she became nervous, scared, or excited. Depending on her level of anxiety, Kae would inadvertently toss in a few expletives. Thus, Kae tipped her hand with this statement, and Thia knew that Kae had been up to something behind her back.

Thia had found out about Kae's tell some years ago, when they scrubbed into the OR as medical students. As soon as the patient on the table, started to lose pressure, the now

74

Dr. Beck (Kae) turned to the nurse and said, "Haul ass and hang that next bag of blood!" The attending surgeon looked at Kae in disgust and she soon calmed down, considering that she wasn't in charge and was still just a student.

The medical staff in the OR laughed for the rest of the week. Kae tried to keep her emotions in check, but everyone agreed that maybe surgery wasn't her forte. Staying calm was a lot easier in the office than in an OR.

Coming back to the present, Thia demanded to know what Kae knew.

"Those buttons aren't buttons. I had them analyzed, and they're composed of a synthetic opioid that's a thousand times more potent than fentanyl. It's a wonder we didn't get high just from touching them!"

"Well, I knew the suitcase contained contraband, I just didn't know where it was until you dissolved the buttons! Now I just need to get it back through security, at the airport."

"Whaaat?! Why are you smuggling drugs?"

Thia started from the beginning of what now seemed to be a terrible nightmare. Upon the story's completion, she sighed, somewhat relieved to be able to tell someone about the predicament she was in.

"Well, we've got twenty-four hours to come up with a plan."

"Why twenty-four hours? I don't return to Chicago until the end of the week."

Kae responded slowly, dragging out each letter of the first word, "Well, the detective who had the button analyzed told me that he would need to report the findings to his superior since the analysis revealed that the button is an illegal substance."

"See? I knew that if you got involved, things would become more complicated. Before, I had a week to figure something out. Now it's only twenty-four hours."

"That's where you wrong. This is complicated, but not impossible." Kae threw in a few profane expletives that revealed her state of anxiety.

Thia didn't know if she could trust Kae's plan since her linguistics hadn't returned to the polished communication that Kae had perfected after many years of education and culture. Kae was still clearly on the verge of some level of hysteria, but without a plan of her own, Thia was prepared to listen.

Kae, sounding more composed, began: "I can go back to the detective and tell him the whole story, just as you've told me. But I'll tell him that the friend I told him about was actually me. That will buy us some time. In the meantime, they'll probably put me under surveillance, hoping to catch the thugs who accosted you. But it won't tip your hand because the police will be nowhere near you. We can only assume that these people have been watching you the whole time you've been here."

Thia briefly recalled the strange woman who was at the waffle house.

"Then what? I'll still be involved in drug trafficking, and if I don't cooperate, they'll implicate me in another crime."

"Trust me! I'll think of something. Until then, we'll only communicate by text in case the police also want me to wear a wire. We won't see each other again until the day you depart, at the airport. We have to find a way to make sure you get your personal effects back and the true criminals are caught."

The next few days were a blur. Thia agreed to Kae's plan because she had nothing else to offer as an alternative. She was trusting Kae, but wondering whether Kae might have seen too many crime shows. What if this plan was the product of some ill-fated forensics-related episode she had watched recently?

Every day, Kae texted Thia between patients to make sure she was okay. As she'd predicted, she was placed under surveillance, but she convinced Detective Geffer that she couldn't wear a wire since it would breach physician-patient confidentiality while she performed her job.

Geffer had agreed to let Kae complete the plan of getting the drugs through airport security and getting "her" IDs and other cards back before confronting and taking down the thugs.

Now that Thia knew and understood the contents of the suitcase, she made sure she knew its whereabouts at all times. She stayed in the hotel room daily, watching the maids clean the room and not leaving until they were done. When she wasn't in the room, she put the "Do not disturb" sign on the door to discourage staff from entering the room in her absence. She actually wanted to take the suitcase everywhere she went, but decided this might draw too much attention to it.

To take her mind off of the contraband, she signed up for a city tour the day before she was scheduled to leave. It didn't matter that she knew most of the city. She needed a distraction.

The same strange woman who had been at the waffle house was in the line, waiting to board the tour bus. Deciding this wasn't a coincidence, Thia immediately ducked out of line at the last minute and rushed back to her hotel room, where she stayed the remainder of the day.

Calling Kae, she advised her of the encounter, wanting to make sure their final plans were intact and that both of them would be safe at the end of the drug exchange, rather than labeled as criminals.

Kae explained very carefully to Thia that they would both arrive at the airport exactly two hours before her flight's departure. They would synchronize their watches. The police would be tailing Kae, and Thia would go through security as planned. Once she got her cards and driver's license, she would signal Kae, who promised to take it from there. Thia wasn't sure she knew what that meant and didn't like the sound of it, but had no choice.

The next day, Thia awakened two hours before her alarm clock was scheduled to go off. She showered, and ate very little. Her stomach hurt and she felt nauseated. Her carry-on was already packed and the ill-fated brown suitcase was sitting next to it. Thia had decided that, from here on out, she would never fall asleep in an airport again, or in any other public place. At 5:00 a.m., the time they'd planned for her to depart from the hotel, she called Kae. They set their watches to match. Between thirty and forty-five minutes later, when she arrived at the airport, they would connect again by text.

When Kae left home by Uber, leaving her beloved car behind, she knew that an officer was somewhere close behind. She advised Thia not to go through security after check-in until she saw Kae come through the doors and get into the security line. This way Kae would be only a few passengers behind Thia.

This was puzzling to Thia. How would Kae be able to continue tailing her through security without a ticket or boarding pass? Well, she just had to trust her. It was too late to ask questions now. Waiting in the area just ten feet from the TSA security checkpoint, Thia was pointedly nervous.

Ten minutes later, Kae arrived. They briefly made eye contact as Thia headed toward the TSA checkpoint. Kae got into line. Only four passengers separated them, which eased Thia's anxiety slightly. As the line snaked its way slowly toward the security agent, Thia had her ticket and passport in hand. Usually, she used her license, but the thugs had stolen it. Lucky for her, that day they went through her carry-on, her passport had been in her back jeans pocket, which she was sitting on. As the line moved forward, a drug-sniffing German shepherd was being guided among the passengers as part of a routine check. The dog diligently sniffed each passenger, briefly stopping at Thia's luggage, but moving on. Relief flooded Thia's body as she prepared to continue through security. Things might work out after all, she thought. She knew it wouldn't be over until she actually cleared security and got her IDs and credit cards back.

As she completed these thoughts, she looked back to see panic cross Kae's face—the dog was headed back, directly toward Thia. Why was this happening? What had made the dog turn around?

"Come with me, ma'am," the agent said as the dog renewed his interest in the suitcase. Thia left the line and was taken to an area off to the side, where the contents of her carry-on were dumped on the counter. "What's going on, officer?"

"We have a new policy of randomly searching suitcases of passengers traveling from areas with high concentrations of drug trafficking. So you've done nothing wrong, you've just been selected for a random search. This still didn't ease Thia's concern. At that moment, she looked up to see the same woman in dark slacks from the waffle house and the tour area. Now she was here in airport security, lurking in the shadows. Something was desperately wrong. If she was trying to be inconspicuous, she wasn't succeeding, and the fact that she was still wearing the same clothes didn't help. The woman stood in the corner, quietly observing the events that transpired.

The security officer took Thia to a small room. They opened her carry-on luggage, followed by the brown suitcase, then dumped the contents onto the counter and rifled through them. "Nothing here," the agent announced to the next agent as they herded her into another area to repack the luggage. "Have a nice day, ma'am!"

Just as Thia was repacking the clothing, she noticed that one of the buttons had a small amount of powder starting to leak from the buttonhole. Panicking, she quickly stuffed the contents into the suitcase and looked around for Kae. Somehow Kae had passed through security uneventfully and was sitting on a bench opposite the checkpoint.

Suddenly the German shepherd whirled around, pulling the leash out of the TSA officer's hand. Running at full speed, the dog jumped up and tackled Thia to the ground. The suitcase fell open and the dog snatched the shirt that had the leaking powder. As the TSA officer caught up, Thia managed to regain her composure. The officer tugged the shirt from the dog's mouth. He called the police on his radio, and they arrived shortly.

"Assuming this is a controlled substance, miss, you are under arrest for possession." The officers snapped her into a pair of handcuffs and seized the suitcase and her other luggage.

At that moment, two large men who had been walking toward Thia did an about-face and rapidly headed in the other direction. Thia wasn't sure whether or not these were the people she was to hand over the case to. At this point, it no longer mattered.

As the police were taking her away, Thia saw Kae staring in disbelief. "Hey . . . Hey, what are you doing?!" Kae was running toward the detainment area. Thia violently shook her head, trying to dissuade Kae from getting involved. "No, Kae! Go get help!"

Kae, frantic with fear, looked around for Detective Geffer and the undercover staff who were supposed to be shadowing her, but they were nowhere to be found. She turned around just in time to see two officers push Thia into a squad car.

Running back outside to the other side of security, Kae saw Detective Geffer and two plainclothes officers with two large, surly-looking men. In that instant, Kae recognized them as the two men who had walked away when Thia was arrested.

"Detective Geffer . . . they have Thia." Breathless from running and fear, Kae continued. "What happened? You told me everything would be okay!"

"Slow down! Who has Thia?"

"The police! They took her away after a drug-sniffing dog tackled her."

"No doubt they detected the contraband that was in the brown suitcase you described."

"What are we going to do? You can't let them charge her. After all, we came to you for help."

"Calm down. I'll find out what precinct they took her to and we'll try to get this straightened out."

Turning to the other officer, he said, "John, take those two down to the station and start the paperwork on them. I'll finish it up later." Detective Geffer's orders were immediately put into effect. Kae knew that Geffer had a high level of authority, but she didn't know if it was enough to save Thia's bacon.

"Why are they under arrest?"

"They had your friend's credit cards and ID, which confirms the story that they forced her into smuggling drugs through security. We saw them following her as she arrived and decided to see what they were up to. Just as TSA called the cops, they started to flee and that's when we pursued them."

"But how are we going to keep them from charging her with possession?"

"Don't worry. I'll take care of it." Detective Geffer's confidence was reassuring. Kae had known the detective for the better part of three years, but never felt comfortable calling him by his first name. He was old enough to be her dad, and this alone warranted respect. They met when she filed a police report regarding fraudulent use of her DEA number. He helped track down the culprits and turned the case over to the DEA. Since then, she had regarded him as her personal hero.

"Why don't you go home?"

"I can't. I told Thia everything would be fine, and it's not. I told her to trust me. I won't be able to relax until I know she's okay. So whatever you need to do, please let me hang around in case I can help!" Kae was surprised at her own composure. She hadn't used any profanity, and as far as she could tell, her grammar was still consistent with the king's English. Thia would be proud.

"Okay, let me find out what precinct she's at. We'll go down there and I'll explain what happened to put her in this situation. But you can't say anything. Let me handle it!"

Upon their arrival, Detective Geffer greeted some of the other officers, whom he apparently knew. He was ushered into the captain's office while Kae stayed in the waiting area. After an hour, he arrived back in the waiting area with Thia in tow.

Tearfully, Kae grabbed Thia in a ferocious bear hug.

"Hold on . . . let me take a deep breath!" Thia was laughing, partly out of nervous fear since she still felt as if this nightmare hadn't completely ended. "Let's get out of here!"

Kae and Thia never knew what transpired between Detective Geffer and the precinct captain, but apparently he was able to convince them of Thia's innocence. He reassured her that she wasn't in any trouble.

Thia wanted Detective Geffer to know that the two men who were arrested at the airport might have a third accomplice. "A woman in a pair of cheap black slacks and white shirt keeps tailing me. She's not inconspicuous, and she might be part of the gang involved in this drug-smuggling scheme."

"Oh, you mean Gertie Green. She's no threat. She just likes to hang out in the local areas, doing what she calls 'citizen patrol.' We humor her, but she's no real threat to anyone. She retired from the force years ago and insists on continuing to 'be of service.' So she watches people who she thinks are of interest, and then calls in anonymous tips. But they really aren't anonymous since everyone in the department knows it's her."

Thia, satisfied with this explanation, directed her focus to a more pressing matter. "What about my flight?"

"Don't worry. We'll make sure you get another flight out just as soon as all the paperwork is completed. After all, you two are heroes. Those buttons are so potent that, in the wrong hands, they could end up killing who knows how many people."

At that moment, Thia relaxed for the first time since she had left home. She needed a vacation from her vacation, but this one would be spent at home with a good book!

Heaven's Gate

MORTALITY

ETERNITY

Heaven's Gate

J ordan Hines was eighty years old. When his doctor advised him that he was dying, it was no surprise that he had more yesterdays than tomorrows. What was a surprise to him was that he had a terminal illness. He had taken care of his health all his life. He always ate the right things, he never smoked or drank, and now his body had betrayed him. Looking back on all the things he could have and might have done, he still felt as if he had made the right choices.

Now, reflecting from a hospital bed, he wondered if there was anything left unsaid or undone. He had spoken with his nieces and nephews to let them know he was ill and in hospice. He didn't go into a lot of detail because he didn't want to dwell on something that couldn't be changed. Since he had no children, the bulk of his estate was going to the church, and the remainder to his nieces and nephews. His brother and sister were already deceased. He was in constant pain, and the majority of his days were spent taking pills and injections for comfort.

Occasionally he would watch TV or listen to his old iPod with radio, but most of the time he was too sleepy from medications to pay close attention.

His nights were interrupted by staff checking to see if he needed anything before they changed shifts. So when he awakened Friday night, he assumed that the presence in his room was the night nurse checking in before she left. The irony was that none of them could give him what he wanted—restful sleep. He had been admitted to inpatient hospice to adjust his pain meds and would be out soon to continue comfort care in his own home. However, he had been awakening around midnight, for the past three nights. He wasn't in pain and there was no activity on the floor, so he couldn't explain the insomnia.

This night was different. Again he awakened at midnight, but there was a warmth in his room that he couldn't explain. He was always cold in his hospital room, no matter how many heated blankets the staff placed on him. But in this very moment, he felt warm and cozy. Just then he heard a voice, or he thought he did. He was on so many meds, maybe he was dreaming or hallucinating.

The voice commanded, "Fear not, Jordan!" Could this be an angel? Jordan was sure he was dreaming because he of all people wouldn't need to be advised of his future.

However, he couldn't help but entertain the thought since, as a Bible scholar, he knew that this was a common greeting to allay the fears of a person being visited by heavenly beings.

"Hello? C-Can I help you?" Jordan stammered, not quite sure how to react or respond to a voice he wasn't sure was there. He didn't see anything, but he felt the presence of someone.

"Fear not!" the voice stated again, this time a little impatiently.

"Okay, so I hear you, but I can't see anything!"

"I am your guardian angel and have been with you all of your life, but as my last act of assistance, I've come to advise you that you are going to heaven, but you will not receive a crown," before the angel could continue, Jordan interrupted.

"What did I do wrong?...where did I mess-up?" Jordan's mind was racing.

"You didn't mess up, per se. But you failed to lead anyone else to salvation. You were saved to save others, and you haven't led anyone else to Christ!"

At this point, Jordan sank to a new level of despair. He didn't think he could feel any worse than when he was given his diagnosis, but this was a new low.

Then he recalled the Bible verse, "Go ye into all the world, and preach the gospel to every creature," in Mark 16:15. Yes, he had gone into the world, but he'd spent most of that time focusing on his own needs. When his wife had died ten years ago, he'd become even more introverted. Well, it was too late now—he was on his deathbed, and in no condition to go into all the world.

The angel, sensing his despair, gave him a few seconds to lament. But, not wanting him to suffer too much longer, he advised Jordan of a chance to make up for lost opportunities. "You are being given three additional chances to witness and lead someone else to salvation."

Without any further explanation, the warmth soon disappeared from the room and Jordan knew the angel was gone. He still had a multitude of questions, but they were left unanswered.

The next night Jordan fell asleep without much difficulty. He drifted off into what felt like a dream, but was all too real. He felt different. Looking into a glass window, he saw his reflection, a younger version of himself. The setting was vaguely familiar. He was in a drugstore. He then recalled a robbery that had occurred thirty years earlier, in this very pharmacy. He had just arrived in the store when he saw a young male shoplifting. Rather than inform the manager or confront the perpetrator, he left the store. The next day, he recalled the newspaper headline detailing a robbery with two casualties. He was happy to have left before the actual crime had taken place. He often felt he had dodged a bullet.

Jordan was back in this same pharmacy, in the cold medication aisle, when he saw the same young man from thirty years before, stuffing Sudafed and other meds into his pockets. This time, instead of walking out, Jordan started talking to the guy. "Hey, young man, do you need money?"

The robber turned around, quite surprised and angry. "Mind your own business!"

"I can pay for whatever you need." Jordan slowly approached the perpetrator.

"What do you care? I need medications for my cold, food, rent money, and car payment money, and I'm in debt to the point of never getting out! So what can you do for me?"

Jordan countered with a question that caught the thief by surprise: "Do you know where you are going?"

"What do you mean?"

"If you died this very minute, do you know where you would spend eternity?"

"There is no eternity or hereafter. When you die, that's it. There's nothing."

"Can I give you something?" Jordan reached into his pocket and, much to his surprise, he had a Christian tract. "Let me give you something to read. There is an afterlife, and we will be accountable for all of our sins and mistakes. But there's someone who can forgive us of our sins, and has paid the price for them. So no matter what else happens, here today and now, you can have eternal life."

"I don't have time for this. Move out of my way! I'm going to rob this place!" The perpetrator grabbed a gun out of his pocket and pushed past Jordan, who followed and tackled him from behind. They struggled with the gun, which accidentally went off, alarming the customers.

During the fight, a police officer rushed down the aisle. "Hands up, both of you!" The robber dropped the gun and reached for the ceiling. Jordan was slow to raise his hands since he felt he shouldn't be considered a suspect. But the officer, looking at him and not knowing the circumstances, advised Jordan to raise his hands for the second time.

"What's going on? I'm Officer Scott."

A lady from another aisle who had called 911 ran to the medication aisle. "I called. I heard them talking and when the young man stated he was going to rob this pharmacy, I called 911. You got here really quick!"

The officer thanked her. "I was next door, wrapping up a previous call, when I got your call. There must be a full moon because a lot is happening in this area tonight!" The officer was cuffing the would-be robber, as he responded to the lady's questions.

Jordan was perplexed and asked the officer if he could have a few more minutes with the young man.

"Look, I don't want to talk to you!" the robber objected. "You're the reason I got caught. If I hadn't been talking to you, I'd got the money, and been gone!"

As the officer escorted the young man out, Jordan felt dejected and wondered what he might have done differently. The one thing that made him feel better was that this time there had been no casualties.

When Jordan awakened, his breakfast was cold and waiting on the bedside table.

"Doc, you feel okay? You slept pretty late today," the nurse queried.

"I feel fine. I'm just a little tired." Actually, Jordan was tired from the emotional letdown of his failure to make an impact on the young man, whose life would be changed forever by a failed attempted robbery. But at least the robbery was foiled and no one was killed.

As the nurse left, Jordan experienced a warmth in the room, much like the presence he had felt when his guardian angel first appeared the night before. Jordan, out of the corner of his eye, spotted a glow. Turning to his right to see where the light was coming from, he saw the angel sitting in the bedside chair, eating his breakfast.

"That didn't go well, at all, Jordie!...... This is cold," the angel stated, pointing to the tray. "Have them heat it up while we talk." The angel was drinking Jordan's coffee and eating the dry, slightly burnt toast.

Jordan hesitated before hitting the call light.

"It's okay, only you can see me. Now let's talk about what happened to the young man you were supposed to lead to the straight and narrow path."

Jordan hadn't expected to see the angel again after getting his instructions the night before—not that he didn't have a lot of questions. He also didn't expect to see him eating. From what Jordan could recall of his Bible readings, angels didn't eat.

Reading his mind, the angel responded. "We don't have to eat as humans do, but when we get the chance, it's a most delightful experience . . . usually. However, this hospital food leaves a lot to be desired."

"I thought I did okay. At least no one was killed this time," Jordan responded, redirecting Jerry's attention away from the tray.

"Yes, well, it could have been better. So this time, I'm going to give you some tips. And since this is going to take longer than I thought, you can call me Jerry."

Jordan thought that was an odd name for an angel. He'd never seen an angel named Jerry in the Bible.

Reading his mind again, Jerry said, "That's because I haven't gotten my wings, and if I don't give you some additional direction and tutoring, I won't get them, and you won't get your crown. You gotta be bold, son! For instance when that young man pulled the gun on you in the pharmacy, you should have let him shoot you!"

"The object was for me to lead him to Christ, not get killed," Jordan interjected.

"Didn't I say, 'Fear not'?" Jerry frowned, somewhat annoyed at being interrupted by his subject. "When you're transported back to an event in the past, your mind and spirit are there, but physically you are still in bed. So if he had shot you, and nothing happened, you would have appeared invincible. Now, *that* would have gotten his attention! Oh, he would have listened to anything you had to say after that . . . or ran. Either way, he would have been transformed. All you did was make him angry!"

Jordan decided to try to limit his thoughts since thinking was the same as talking when Jerry could read his mind.

"Now, Jordie, I don't know what your next assignment is going to be, but you've got to think outside the box, man, and remember—my wings and your crown are riding on this. If you don't succeed, I fail as well! And please, stop thinking so much. If you've got something to say, just say it! Be bold, man!"

Addressing Jordan's last thought, Jerry sighed. "No, I don't speak like the angels in the Bible because we're in modern times. We have to adapt to the times. If I had addressed you with thee, thou, art, and so forth, it would take more time for you to grasp what I'm trying to explain."

Jordan had more questions, but before he could ask, the temperature dropped in the room and Jerry was gone.

The only direction Jordan got was to "be bold and think outside the box." He wasn't quite sure what that meant, but it didn't sound safe.

The rest of the day, Jordan sat outside his room, passing out tracts and talking to visitors about Christ and salvation. At least, to those who would listen. Some of them rolled their eyes and looked at him with distrust or just took the tract and kept walking. This had become Jordan's everyday activity since Jerry's revelation that Jordan hadn't led anyone to salvation.

That night when Jordan fell asleep, he went further back in his life, to when he first got married. He was on his honeymoon in Maui. Jordan recognized the resort. He recalled meeting a couple that was friendly enough, but didn't seem to be having a good time. He had originally decided not to pry and remained content to greet them cordially when passing in the hallway or at breakfast.

This time, while sitting at the pool, Jordan engaged the husband in what was initially small talk. It was, however, just enough to get him to open up. He found out that the husband, Todd, and his wife Maria were in a troubled marriage. They were going to professional counseling and were advised by the therapist to take a much-needed vacation to help get their marriage back on track. It turned out that Maria had had an affair with one of the deacons at their church.

Jordan thought that this couple must not be his targeted audience since they were already church members. He continued to talk with Todd, who appeared to need to vent.

Todd lamented, "It's going to take more than a vacation to get us back on track."

Jordan suggested that they consider counseling in the church since they were both Christians.

"I'm not a true believer. I just go to church because my wife is a member. Matter of fact, I've never told her, but I'm an atheist! Besides, why would I want to be counseled by Christians? After all, the guy who ruined our marriage is a Christian."

"Please know that Christians make mistakes, too. The lack of a relationship with God will cost you more than a marriage if you don't repent of your sins and accept Jesus Christ as your Lord and Savior."

"The people in the church are no better than those outside the church," Todd continued as if he hadn't heard a word Jordan said.

Jordan persisted. "Although Christians may still sometimes sin, as your wife did, the difference is that their sins are covered, and they can be forgiven and still have a relationship with Christ. You, on the other hand, as a non-believer, will pay the ultimate price for your sins by going to hell if you remain unsaved."

"I'm just not at that point."

"Okay. Well, can I give you something?" Just as Jordan reached into his pocket, his foot slipped on the wet poolside pavement. He careened forward into the deep end of the pool.

His head slipped below the water. Fluttering and flailing, he felt like he was grasping at straws. Just before his head sank below the water again, he managed to sputter the words "Fire! Fire!"

Just as Jordan was going down again, Todd jumped into the pool. Clutching Jordan around the chest with one arm, he swam a few feet to the edge; by then, someone had thrown in a life preserver. Todd retrieved Jordan from the pool and with the help of another good Samaritan, placed him in the recovery position on his side. Just then, the paramedics arrived. Jordan was placed on oxygen as he was wheeled into the ambulance on a collapsible gurney.

The paramedic turned to Todd. "Are you coming, sir? We need a relative to help give a history."

"No," Jordan spoke up, now more alert. "I can give you a history. I'm tired, not dead."

"I'm going with you until they can notify your wife. I can take a taxi back to the hotel."

"Uber or Lyft would be cheaper—" Jordan stopped, realizing that he was sometime in the 1980s, long before ride-sharing services existed.

"You really aren't making any sense, Jordan. Just relax!"

"Okay, but I have to tell you that when I went under that water for a third time, I thought I was a goner. My life didn't flash in front of my eyes, but I remember thinking that I was so happy that no matter what happened, I was going to be fine!"

"You mean you knew you weren't going to die?"

"No, I knew that if I died, my soul would spend eternity with God."

"That's deep! I'm really starting to rethink our previous conversation. I'd like to have that peace and assurance that you exhibited in the face of danger. Do you still have that tract you were trying to give me when you fell into the water?"

Jordan looked in his pocket, and found some additional tracts that were soaked, but still legible. After squeezing the excess water from one, he handed it to Todd.

"One other question. Why did you yell 'fire' when you fell into the pool?"

Jordan smiled. "I recall seeing a program on personal safety, and the advice was to yell 'fire' when in peril. It was thought that people might tend to respond more to "fire" than to a cry for 'help.'"

* * * * * * *

After the doctors examined Jordan, they advised him that he would be kept overnight. Todd decided to go back to the hotel since Jordan was in good hands.

"Good luck with your marriage. We're in suite 200 if you want to talk some more. Just remember this verse: 'God so loved the world, that he gave his only begotten son, that whosoever believeth in him should not perish, but have everlasting life.' It's in the Bible, in John 3:16."

Jordan fell asleep. When he awakened, he was back in Chicago in his own hospital bed.

"Hey, Jordie, way to go!" Jerry had his hand poised for a high five, but Jordan left him hanging. He was still half asleep.

Jordan pulled himself up in bed to see Jerry drinking his orange juice with one hand and picking up a cheese danish in the other.

Jerry continued, "Man, that was genius. Falling into the pool like that meant you were able to extend your time with Todd and go deeper into the Christian experience and salvation. At first, though, I thought you were trying to walk on water to get his attention or prove a point. By the way, why were you yelling 'fire'?"

Jordan was too angry to answer. His guardian angel was present when he almost drowned and did absolutely nothing. What good was having a guardian angel who knows you are in distress, and doesn't rescue you? To top it off, he thought the angel's focus was more on his breakfast than on him.

"There you go, thinking again. I'm right here. First off, as I told you before, you are not going to be physically harmed during these interventions!"

"Well, it felt very real to me. I thought I was actually going to drown and—" Jordan raised his voice for the first time, not realizing it.

"And yet here you are, back in your bed, snug as a little bug and ready for breakfast."

Jordan looked at the tray that was now completely bare, containing only one crumb from the danish. If there was anything else for his breakfast, he couldn't tell since the plate was otherwise clean.

Jerry replied to Jordan's disgusted look. "You didn't miss anything!"

"Well, I wouldn't know that since there's nothing left!"

"Jordie, Jordie, Jordie. Let's not get hung up on something as minor as food. Let's talk about what I can do to help you. After all, I'm your guardian angel."

"Well, I think I made more of an impact with Todd than I did in the first intervention. He stated that he was actually considering our conversation more seriously after I told him about the peace that comes with knowing where you're going when you die. But he didn't commit to anything."

"And that's okay, Jordie. You made him think. You planted the seed and sometimes that's all you can do. You may not see the harvest!"

Finally, some words of wisdom, Jordan thought. Interestingly enough, Jerry didn't comment on Jordan's thought, but Jordan knew he'd heard it because Jerry smiled and left, fading away.

Minutes later, the medical assistant came into the room to get his tray. "Good morning! Can I take your tray?"

"Yes. Can I get another breakfast? I'm a little hungry this morning."

"Sure. You must be feeling better—I think you ate more in the last two days than you did in the first three!"

Jordan hadn't thought about it, but he also hadn't been in any pain since Jerry had been present. He knew it couldn't be the pain meds because he hadn't needed to request them since the first encounter with Jerry. That's odd, he thought. Maybe Jerry was good for something other than eating.

That night Jordan fell asleep with high expectations. He went to sleep reading his Bible. He felt energized and determined to succeed; this was his last chance.

This night, he was transported to a more recent time. He recognized the setting as a family Christmas dinner. These events had been taking place at his sister's home for the majority of his adult life, and for the most part, they were fairly enjoyable. This year was different due to the loss of his nephew, Gregory, who had been the victim of an accidental shooting several months prior. There was a heaviness in the air that, despite the gaiety of the Christmas music and good food, couldn't be shaken. Jordan's nephew was well loved, but the bullet that stopped him in his tracks didn't care about that, or about the promising future before him.

Gregory was only twenty-two years old when a stray bullet traveled through his living room and struck him in the chest. His girlfriend Dana was watching TV with him when it happened. In shock, she didn't speak for a whole month, afterward. She was angry with everyone. Friends and relatives kept advising her to pray, but she didn't know how to begin. She wasn't an atheist, per se, but she hadn't thought much about God. Now, she decided that there couldn't be a God because good people all around her were dying. Dana decided she couldn't go to Gregory's family dinner that year. She was still depressed and knew that being around his family would make her feel worse. Gregory's mother called and insisted she come.

"I'll stop by, but only for a short time." Dana had spent every Christmas with Greg's family, since they had met. Without him it would seem strange, but mostly sad. She was determined to make an appearance for his mom's sake.

When she arrived at the door, she was greeted by Jordan, Greg's uncle. "Hey, Dana! Come on in!"

Jordan wasn't sure who was supposed to be his intended target. All of his family members were saved. So he decided to let the evening unfold. Dana was probably saved too, he thought, since Greg had been very spiritual and had been baptized at the age of nine.

At the table, before the meal, everyone was asked to say what they were thankful for. Much to everyone's surprise, Dana passed.

After dinner, Jordan noticed that Dana was unusually quiet. "Are you all right, Dana?"

"I'm good, but why are you all so grateful? Gregory is gone! We'll never hear him laugh or see his smile again."

"Yes, Dana, but we'll be with Gregory in eternity. He was saved at the age of nine. And you'll see him, too."

"I don't believe in any life after death. I don't believe in a God who lets good people die."

"God doesn't let people die. He allows us free will, and that sometimes results in death and violence. We as Christians have an obligation to try to effect change and promulgate goodness in the earth realm. And no matter what happens to the physical body, our souls will go to live with God. You can have this same assurance if you accept Jesus Christ as your Lord and Savior."

Dana rolled her eyes and walked away, but Jordan wasn't discouraged. "Let me give you this tract. Read it and tell me what you think about it. We'll be here all day, and we can talk some more."

"You mean *you'll* be here all day! I'm going to a club to meet some friends!"

Just then, Jordan's wife walked over. She noticed that her husband was spending an awful lot of time with Dana. As she suspected, Jordan was concerned about Dana's state of mind.

"Did you know she isn't a believer?" Jordan queried his wife.

"No. I assumed that she was saved because she was with Gregory. It must be very difficult for her without faith to fall back on. Don't worry, she's young. She has time to get it right."

But *I* don't have time, Jordan thought. He knew Dana was his last chance to save someone in order to gain his crown. As he tried to follow Dana, his wife pulled him back.

"Jordan, you can't force your beliefs on others. Let her read the tract, and then see how she feels!"

Jordan couldn't tell his wife about his assigned tasks. She'd only think he'd had too much of his sister's rum-spiked eggnog. One good thing about going back to previous life events was that he got to see his wife, who had died ten years before he was diagnosed with cancer. He also saw his sister, who was now deceased, too.

Since he had failed for a third time, he decided to enjoy the rest of the evening with his deceased wife. Heading back to the kitchen, Jordan couldn't believe his eyes. In the corner, a warm light was hovering over the spaghetti and meatballs. With a fork in one hand and a glass of punch in the other, Jerry was eating directly out of the serving dish.

"Really? Really?!" Jordan was dumbfounded. "I thought you couldn't participate in interventions."

"I'm not participating. No one knows I'm here! I'm eating!" Jerry responded. Focusing again on the task at hand, Jerry gave Jordan more advice. "You know, your sister makes a mean chocolate cake. It's going fast; make sure you get some of it before it's gone! And quit worrying—like I told you before, only you can see me."

"Well, the way you're bingeing, she'll know someone was back here eating her out of house and home."

"Yes, and that someone will be you, because she'll only see you!"

Jordan gave up. When it came to food, there was no reasoning with Jerry. He went back to the living room to join the rest of the family. They were watching a game between the Los Angeles Lakers and the Chicago Bulls.

The next morning Jordan awakened, tired and dejected. He waited for the nurse to assist him with getting up so the assistant could help him bathe. After breakfast he patiently waited for the doctor. The new pain regimen was working, and its name was Jerry. Since Jerry had visited that first night, Jordan hadn't been in any pain.

"Good morning, doc," Jordan greeted his attending, wanting very much to go home.

"Mr. Hines, you can go home tomorrow, but I want to observe you for one more day to make sure we have your pain under control. Have you been sleeping well?"

Jordan was a little perturbed that the doctor didn't address him as Dr. Hines, but he acknowledged that he had been retired some fifteen years plus.

"Yes." Jordan knew answering any other way might lead to him staying longer. He knew the game of how to get discharged. After all, he had discharged many a patient from the hospital himself.

Jordan decided to make the most of the rest of his stay, continuing to pass out tracts. He positioned himself at his door and continued to talk to visitors and patients who passed by, asking the age-old, thought-provoking question. "Do you know where you will spend eternity?" Most of the individuals just smiled or ignored him. Nevertheless, several of them did take the tracts.

At midday his nurse stopped by to wish him good luck since she would be off the next day, when he was scheduled to be discharged.

"Hi, Dr. Hines. Just wanted to let you know what a pleasure it has been taking care of you since I won't be here when you're discharged tomorrow."

"Thank you. I appreciate what you and Dr. Brown have done to make me comfortable and to give me the best care possible."

"You're welcome! You know, he almost discharged you yesterday because some of the patients and visitors were starting to complain about your passing out tracts. One patient went so far as to say that you asked her guests if they knew they were going to hell. Of course, I know you'd never say anything like that, but people tend to exaggerate when you strike a nerve."

Jordan was shocked. "No, I never said those words to anyone. I was trying to witness in the best way I knew how. But I guess it wasn't appreciated."

"Well, Dr. Hines, don't stop! And if you need anything, feel free to call us here at the hospital. But I know Dr. Brown will take good care of you."

The next morning Jordan was delivered home by a medical car. He settled in and slept well that night. The following morning, the visiting hospice nurse arrived, but no one answered the door. Using the key Jordan had given her, she found him quietly nestled in bed and tried to rouse him by shaking him. When she found no pulse, she knew he was gone.

Jordan awakened in a tunnel of warm bright light. At the end of it, he was met by his guardian angel, Jerry. Without a beverage or food in his hand, Jordan almost didn't recognize him.

"Welcome, Jordie! Why the long face?"

Jordan looked up and smiled, addressing the warm light hovering overhead. "I'm happy to be here, but I failed miserably!" Jordan looked around at the most beautiful place he had ever imagined. It was beyond description. "I guess I wasn't meant to wear a crown."

Jerry led him to a large pond. As he peered into it, he saw his reflection. Over his head was a golden halo of light encrusted with multiple gems: rubies, diamonds, sapphires, and more, some the likes of which Jordan had never seen. He marveled at the beauty of the crown, which was weightless.

The angel responded to his thoughts. "That's right Jordan, the crown is weightless; it's a reward, not a burden."

"But I wasn't able to save any of the people I witnessed to." Jordan was puzzled.

"You planted the seeds, but the harvest came later. The robber, also known as Jerome, went to prison, and thanks to you he started a prison ministry and became a minister after he was released. Todd, the disgruntled husband, returned to church with his wife for counseling. He didn't save his marriage, but he was saved and witnessed to others, who were converted."

107

Just then Jordan saw a crowd of people heading toward him, led by his wife. Included in the crowd were the robber and Todd.

"What about Dana?" Jordan queried.

"She hasn't come home yet. She did convert, and she leads a Christian ministry for young millennials. She is planting the seed of faith in many. So you see, Jordan, your efforts weren't in vain. And who knows, those tracts you've been passing out may have found their way to fertile ground."

Jordan looked at Jerry, who wasn't wearing wings.

Jerry responded, "Oh, yeah, they had to be refitted. The ones that were originally ordered didn't fit once they arrived. I guess I might have put on a few pounds!"

"You think?" Jordan smiled, happy to be home.

Lightning Strikes

CHICAGO

ADVENTURE

GREED

KIDNAPPING

SIBLING RIVALRY

Lightning Strikes

Damian wasn't looking forward to his third year of high school. Most of his classmates were excited about the prospect of becoming upperclassmen, but even with this promotion, Damian knew he would still be subject to bullying. Because of stuttering he was mocked and belittled by other students. He had pleaded with his mother to allow him to be homeschooled when he was younger, but she had argued that once he was in high school, things would be different since the students would be more mature, with more important things to focus on.

Much to Damian's dismay, this was not the case. The ill-treatment had continued daily for the next two years. Slowly Damian had begun to withdraw socially and to keep his head down. During class he was attentive and took good notes. He let his written work speak for him. Thus far he was getting A's and B's, so he couldn't complain and neither could his mom. However, Damian knew that if he didn't have to contend with the bullying, he would probably be getting all A's since some of his classes required classroom participation, which he no longer engaged in.

He'd entered his sophomore year thinking things might be different, but they weren't, so he had little hope, for this year. The bane of his existence was Troy Thorne, a bigger-than-life bully who, as a five-year-old, was the terror of the playground. Always around to remind Damian of his speech impediment, Troy had terrorized him through grammar school and the first two years of high school. If he would just go away—change schools, move, anything—Damian would be ecstatic. However, Troy continued to be ever-present, growing bigger each year. Good grief, what is his mom feeding him? Damian wondered; one could only imagine. His growth spurt seemed to have started at birth, and he was a virtual Goliath among his peers. Damian had been shoved by Troy several times when he had tried to defend himself, but thank goodness it had never led to an all-out fight because Damian was sure he would have lost, at the very least, or even suffered physical harm.

The first day of junior year was a clear, crisp autumn day. Fall was in the air and the leaves were all hues of brown, orange, and bright scarlet. Damian marveled at the changes of nature as a distraction from his upcoming emotional trauma. As the first class bell rang, various groups of students who were huddled outside the school entrance milled toward the door. These represented different social groups that had become friends over the past two years. Based on common interests, there were the jocks, the cheerleaders, the nerds, the class clowns, and others. There was no group of stutterers, so Damian just gravitated to the "other" group. They weren't truly friends, but they tolerated each other out of necessity. Damian knew the names of all the people in his loosely formed crew.

Gary was probably the guy he had the most in common with. Gary didn't stutter, but he was still not accepted due to his "nerd" status. He was a good chess player, and Damian hadn't found anyone to match his skill level. Even Damian's dad was impressed with his son, whom he taught to play chess at the tender age of five. He still hadn't beaten his dad, but it was taking his dad longer to win.

Damian and Gary were only in one class together, so for most of the day, Damian went from class to class feeling alone and dejected. They were both in AP Calculus, so he felt less like an outsider during third period, when he and Gary could trade notes and sneak knowing glances while other classmates solved problems incorrectly at the blackboard. Damian didn't mind participating in calculus since the solution to a math problem required very little speech and the work spoke for itself. He enjoyed this respite because from fourth period on, he didn't participate in class unless he was called on. English, US history, computer science, etc., went like a blur. If Damian forgot and raised his hand to answer, he had to brace himself for the snickers that would go on and on after it took him several minutes to utter what should have been a thirty-second response. Damian knew that he would also have to run to the Fifty-Ninth Street bus stop to try to get the 4:00 p.m. bus. If he missed it, he would have to wait forty-five minutes to catch the next one. By then the majority of the eighth- and ninth-period students were dismissed from class. If he was the only "other" waiting, he got quips and harassment that could last throughout the thirty-minute ride home.

"D-D-D-Damian, how was class? D-d-d-did you get the A for the d-d-day? W-w-what you g-g-got on?" This could last for the duration of the ride. If Damian tried to defend himself verbally, the harassment worsened. The events sometimes deteriorated into a shoving match or, worse yet, a fight. So Damian tried to resist the urge to respond by staying quiet.

He had discussed homeschooling with his parents, but they wouldn't have any part of it. They thought the bullying was a phase that was supposed to build his character. Damian didn't see it and thought they were being unreasonable.

This trip seemed unusually long. Finally, Damian arrived at his stop. Troy jumped up and blocked the exit as Damian prepared to leave the bus.

The girls on the bus giggled as the guys egged him on.

"That's right, Troy, he paid to get on. Make him pay to get off. There are no free lunches!"

Damian pushed past him and ran through traffic to get to the opposite side. Troy, energized by the jeers of the other students, jumped off the bus in pursuit. Upon reaching the curb, Damian heard a loud thud and car brakes screeching. He looked back to see Troy curled up on the pavement in pain. The bus driver stopped the bus and jumped out in the middle of stopped traffic. While the driver checked on Troy, Damian called 911 from his cell.

"Son, are you okay?" the bus driver looked concerned as he kneeled over Troy. Troy groaned and looked at Damian and the driver, in obvious pain. "What were you thinking, running into traffic like that?!" The driver shook his head.

"Yeah, he came out of nowhere; thank goodness I was able to stop quickly!" the car driver was visibly shaken.

Damian knew the answer to that question but decided this was not the time to discuss Troy's intent in following him.

When the ambulance arrived, all the other students were gathered around Troy, taking in the situation. "Troy, you okay? Are you hurt? What happened?" A myriad of questions came from the crowd of students who had gotten off of the bus.

"Everyone, move back!"

The paramedics made their way through the crowd. Troy was lifted onto the gurney and it was elevated, rolled, and placed inside the ambulance. By now he was fully awake and looking around, somewhat dazed.

Sydney, a girl from AP Calculus, looked at Damian with suspicion. "What happened, Damian? What did you do?"

Damian was dumbfounded. "What d-d-did I do? I g-g-got off the bus. You all saw m-m-me g-g-get off, d-d-despite Troy trying to block my exit." The more upset Damian became, the worse his stuttering got. He decided to stop defending himself. After all, everyone had seen what happened, and although Troy was the one who got hit, Damian felt as if he was the real victim. Troy had just experienced karma.

Damian walked the remaining block home, wondering if Troy was going to be okay. "Hey, Mom," he yelled as he entered the house. "Guess w-w-what happened to Troy? He was hit by a car!"

"Oh, Damian, that's awful," Ms. Joy said. "Was he hurt badly?"

"D-d-don't know. The ambulance t-t-took him away, but he w-w-was awake when they p-p-put him in th-th-the ambulance."

"What happened, Damian?"

"I'm not sure. I g-g-got off of the bus. M-m-my back was turned when I heard c-c-car b-b-brakes screech as I reached the curb. It wasn't his st-st-stop, so I'm n-n-not sure why he g-g-got off of the b-b-bus at that time." Damian knew why Troy had gotten off the bus, encouraged by the bloodthirsty jeers of the other students. But he decided not to tell. Besides, whenever he had told his parents about these encounters before, they saw them as character-building. Why would this be any different?

Over the next few days, Damian was still bullied, but the intensity was less. It appeared that some of the bullies were distracted by Troy's accident. It may have been that some of them saw it as bad karma for coming after Damian. Whatever the case, Damian was happy for a partial reprieve.

Word had filtered back to school that Troy was okay. He had been sent home from the hospital after two days with only a few bumps and bruises.

The third day after Troy's accident, Ms. Joy met Damian at the door upon his arrival home. "Damian, why didn't you tell me that Troy was chasing you off the bus when he got hit? This bullying is getting out of hand."

"How d-d-did you f-f-find out?"

"One of the students on the bus told Principal Smith. She called me to find out if I knew what had happened from your perspective."

"W-w-well, he didn't actually ch-ch-chase me, from wh-wh-what I could tell. But he d-d-did try to b-b-block my exit as I g-g-got off the bus. I crossed through t-t-traffic and reached th-

116

th-the curb. The next th-th-thing I knew, I h-heard screeching br-br-brakes behind m-m-my back. I d-d-didn't actually see th-th-the accident itself."

"Ms. Smith says the kids told her that Troy had been bullying you before he pursued you off of the bus."

Damian noticed that the emphasis was all on Troy. The other students failed to mention their own participation. But he didn't say anything.

"Well, we have to put an end to this. I've called Troy's mother. The four of us are going to meet and work this out. After all, it could've been you who was hit. You know better than to cross the street through traffic. Why didn't you go to the corner? What were you thinking?"

Damian didn't bother to respond to this last question since he knew it didn't warrant a response.

He really didn't want his mom involved directly in this quandary. If it didn't work, he would then be perceived as a "momma's boy" or "whiner." He was convinced the only solution that would allow him to save face was homeschooling. However, his mother had already decided that this meeting was happening. Damian knew from history that there was no changing her mind.

The meeting was set for the day before Troy was scheduled to return to school. Ms. Joy and Ms. Thorne were determined to get their sons on the same page before they met at school again. Troy and Ms. Thorne were invited to the Joys' for afternoon sandwiches and soda. Damian didn't understand why they had to meet. To him, the solution was simple: Troy and the other kids just needed to leave him alone. Live and let live.

Upon the Thornes' arrival, Ms. Joy greeted them at the door. Damian sat at the kitchen table, not quite prepared for the way these events were unfolding. Both mothers agreed that Damian and Troy would explain in their own words what the problem was.

Troy went first, at Ms. Joy's insistence, since he was the guest.

"Well, Ms. Joy, I have nothing against Damian personally, but he has made himself an outcast at school. We've tried to be friends with him, but he's always ignored us, like he's too good to be bothered with us."

"W-W-Wait a m-m-m-minute!" Damian interrupted, appalled at the turn of events.

"Wait, Damian. Let him finish. Then you can tell your side of the story," Ms. Joy calmed Damian.

"I would like to have Damian as a friend, but he doesn't want to be my friend. He thinks he's better than the rest of us because of his smarts. He's smug and snotty."

"Well, even if you think he snubbed you, what has Damian done to you personally that you think warrants your bullying him, or harassing him, and making fun of his stuttering?" Ms. Joy was puzzled.

Troy responded, "He started the harassment by making fun of my size and calling me a freak."

Damian was stunned by this out-and-out lie.

"Okay, Damian. It's your turn."

"The last two years at school, I've been tortured. I barely have one or two friends, and it's certainly not from lack of trying. I'm ridiculed and bullied at every turn just because I stutter. Every time I open my mouth, it's an opportunity for you or one of your crew to make fun of me and bully me. I've never made fun of you. It would be unfair for me to make fun of any physical attributes that you have no control over. Furthermore, you would welcome a reason to fight me, so why would I consider making fun of you?"

Ms. Joy stood awestruck, mouth open. She had never heard Damian utter more than a word or two without stuttering. Angry at the account that Troy was giving of their relationship, Damian didn't stumble over one word.

"Well, you're not stuttering now." Ms. Thorne looked at Damian in an accusatory manner.

"Trust me, he has a speech impediment that has made him the butt of plenty of jokes and harassment. My son has come home over the years often dejected and in tears because of the cruelty of people like your son."

Damian was happy that his mother was starting to see his point of view, but embarrassed by her account of his being brought to tears.

"Well, his stuttering shouldn't keep him from making friends. Don't blame Troy because your son has poor people skills. We're leaving!"

"Good riddance, and if your son's bullying results in any harm to my son, I'm going to hold you personally responsible as his parent."

The remainder of the evening, Damian and his mother marveled at the miracle. They continued to talk, and Ms. Joy even had Damian read tongue twisters to see if more difficult phrases would result in any faltering or return to stuttering. This didn't happen. It was as if Damian had awakened from a bad dream. The next day, Damian was excited about going to school. He got up early and, upon arriving at school, went straight up to the bullies, including Troy.

"Good morning, peeps. It's a dope day. The sun is shining, the birds are singing! Let's go in and expand our minds!" Damian walked away triumphantly, feeling the eyes of the bullies following him in disbelief.

Gary ran up to Damian hearing this discourse, "Hey, what happened? Have you been fooling us?! Man, that was priceless!"

Damian filled Gary in on the fit of anger that had resulted in the resolution of his stuttering. "Hey, let's celebrate! Let's go to Culver's for lunch instead of the cafeteria."

The rest of the day went by in a whirlwind as Damian felt compelled to participate in all of his classes, raising his hand in response to every question he knew the answer to. His teachers were amazed, and each one asked to talk to him after class.

Weeks went by, and life was great! Kids who had never spoken to him were inviting him to sit with them at lunch and in study hall. However, Damian continued to stick with the "others."

Troy was still in class periodically, but he was no longer a fixture lurking around every corner to traumatize Damian. Damian wondered what insecurity Troy was hiding by focusing on the shortcomings of others.

The bullies soon forgot about Damian. He was no longer getting his locker decorated with the likes of cartoon characters who stuttered. Damian was even considering asking someone to go to junior prom, a prospect he hadn't thought was possible just months before.

Jaynee, whom he had liked since eighth grade, was even starting to acknowledge his nods as they passed in the hallway between classes. He had never actually tried to talk to her for fear that she would tease him for stuttering or, worse yet, tolerate him out of pity. Well, that day had passed. He had gained his voice and he was going to use it.

This bright and wonderful Friday, Damian was going to ask her out, "Hey, Jay—" he started. But as Damian approached her locker, Troy cut in front of him, blocking his path.

"Jaynee, let's hang out after class," Troy said loudly. "I got my dad's car and a bunch of us are going to the movies. Meet me out front after class!"

"Dope!" That was all she said, and it was settled. Turning around, she glanced at Damian, who was just feet from her locker.

"Damian, did you want something?"

"Nah. Have a good one, Jaynee!" The enthusiasm in his voice was there to mask his pain. Did Troy do that on purpose? It was hard to tell, but maybe Damian had been wearing his heart on his sleeve and others could see that he had a thing for Jaynee as well. What if Jaynee knew? He'd die from embarrassment. He wouldn't have the nerve to ask her to prom. He'd just have to wait and see. Maybe on Monday he'd be able to engage her in conversation to see how the dust had settled after her group date with Troy.

On Monday Damian decided to walk home. It was a beautiful April day, an unseasonably warm seventy-eight degrees. The grass was greener than he had ever noticed before. He walked the same route of the Fifty-Ninth Street bus he usually took home. Some of the kids from his school waved from the open windows as they passed. Damian hadn't seen Jaynee between classes that day, so he never got a chance to get the 411 on her date. Damian wasn't really calling it a date since it sounded like a group outing, but he would find out sooner or later. After all, prom was less than two months away and he needed to make plans.

He was just about home when he realized he had left his laptop in his locker. He turned around, heading back toward the school, and called his mom.

"Don't bother, Damian. You can get it tomorrow. I'll drive you to school so you'll be bright and early, and you can submit your homework prior to class."

The next day, on the way to school, Damian played games on his cell phone. Ms. Joy smiled, so happy to see the cloud lifted from her son's life. Words couldn't describe the way she and her husband felt about their son's breakthrough.

As Damian and his mother pulled up, they saw a crowd at the bus stop, across the street from the school. Normally, she would have dropped Damian off, but this time she needed to know why the crowd was there. As they were headed toward the area, one of the students shouted, "Get the principal! Troy has been hit, and the driver sped off. I've called 911!"

For the second time, Damian found himself standing over Troy. The bully's left leg was twisted and, even to a layperson, appeared to be broken.

Ms. Joy placed her sweater over Troy's chest. He was trembling more from the shock than cold. "It will be fine, baby." She put her hand on Troy's forehead, her maternal instincts kicking in as she realized that this could be her son. As the ambulance cleared away the crowd to get to Troy, Ms. Joy marveled silently, what are the odds that someone would be hit twice by a car in a matter of months? It's as if lightning has struck twice! How sad!

Turning to Damian, she made him promise that he would be careful coming and going from school, and any place where he was subject to traffic or other hazards.

The remainder of the school day, all anyone could think about was Troy lying on the ground in pain. Troy texted one of his friends from the hospital to tell them his leg was broken. He was advised that even with surgery, he would probably still have a limp after his leg healed.

Troy returned to school six weeks later, using a crutch for support. He was still in rehab and was expected to be able to eventually walk without it. However, his doctor warned that he would still have a limp. Initially, Troy's buddies were all very sympathetic, volunteering to carry books and other items, holding the door, etc. But as time passed, his friends became less sympathetic and began to avoid him altogether, unable to accept that the old Troy was never going to return. The Troy who towered over everyone at six foot one and played football and rugby, the Troy who was condescending, leading attacks on other students who were less athletic or physically able, or thought to be deficient in other ways, wouldn't be back.

As the next few months passed, Damian took notice of the bullying going on around him. He hadn't been able to notice it before due to his own predicament. Now, as he took stock of the high school landscape, he noticed instances of "shoe shaming" for those who couldn't afford designer gym shoes, fat shaming for some full-figured students, hair shaming, and more.

Damian wondered if there was a way he could make an impact on the culture of Landlin High School. While considering the possibilities, he heard students chanting, "Limpy, limpy, limpy, gimpy!" The syncopated rhythm of this chant sounded painfully familiar. Damian rounded the corner to see Jeff, previously Troy's best friend, leading the mob chant. The other remaining students were people who had been involved in shaming Damian before his stuttering resolved.

Damian decided he had no skin in the game and rounded the corner, going straight to class. Troy was experiencing karma, or bad juju. Who was Damian to argue with what appeared to be poetic justice? This wasn't the first time Damian had happened upon Troy being harassed and bullied, but he had chosen to ignore it.

Several weeks later, Troy was limping to his next class, with taunters following close behind.

Damian, angered and empowered by the situation, walked up to Jeff. "What the hell are you doing?"

124

Surprised by this direct challenge, Jeff looked at Damian in disbelief. "Why should you care? Troy tormented you for years. No one came to your rescue!"

"Exactly. No one cared enough to stop the bullying, and now I'm saying it's enough!" Damian braced himself for what was surely going to be a fight. The other four bullies had since walked away, so Jeff realized it was just him against Damian. He pressed his nose against Damian's and whispered a threat that no one else could hear.

Damian backed up, not appreciating the breech of his personal space. "Don't threaten me, Jeff, unless you're prepared to act on it. Matter of fact, there's no time like the present. Do something now. Jump!"

Jeff backed down from the challenge. In the meantime, Troy limped to fourth-period English. Since the accident, Troy had been stooped over, no longer the imposing bully he once was. Damian made it to his seat just before the bell, surprised at himself. He avoided violence when he was being bullied, but found the courage to endure or inflict violence for someone else who was being verbally attacked.

Damian had been pushed almost to the point of a fight. His thoughts returned to possible solutions to bullying. He decided that the first step was education. The school intercom announcements that were made in the first fifteen minutes of the day were of no consequence to anyone. Damian thought, why not take this time and use it to educate students on relevant topics, such as bullying?

That evening, Damian told his parents about the fight that had almost resulted from defending Troy.

"So, what are you going to do differently the next time you see Jeff?" his dad asked.

"I hope I can avoid a confrontation with him. But there will always be bullies; I'm convinced of it. Troy stopped bullying after his accident, and Jeff was quick to step up and take his place. He turned on Troy, his own best friend. I think the only way to dissuade bullying is to educate people on the topic."

Both Mr. and Ms. Joy smiled broadly, proud of the mature insight Damian had into what had previously been a very painful topic for him.

"But I don't know where to start. How do I get the school to start an education program? I thought about maybe using the school intercom system, but I'm not sure who to ask about that."

"Present your idea to Principal Smith. If she thinks it's good, she may be able to tell you the next steps." Mr. Joy was proud that Damian had changed from being a victim of bullying to trying to eradicate it.

The next day, Damian went to the principal's office. Usually this was a place he tried to avoid, but today he was excited about talking to Ms. Smith. As he waltzed in, he expected to speak to the principal immediately.

The receptionist smiled at him. "How can I help you, young man?"

"I'd like to make an appointment with Principal Smith."

"What is the nature of your business?"

Damian hesitated, not used to this level of formality. "Well, I have an idea to help with bullying, and I'd like to discuss it with the principal."

"Okay, let me look at her schedule. She's very busy, so come prepared and don't waste her time. I suggest that you have your idea written out so she can refer back to it if she needs to. Come back tomorrow at 12:15 p.m. I assume this will be your lunch period."

That night Damian wrote out a plan suggesting the PSA intercom as a vehicle for education on bullying.

He was excited as he approached the principal's office the next day. "Come in, Damian. Ms. Smith is waiting for you."

"Good afternoon, Damian," the principal greeted him. "I've been told you want to address the issue of bullying. I understand that you've had a personal experience with it here at the school. Therefore I have the utmost respect for your views on what might be done about this problem."

Damian's mouth was dry as he presented his idea. He became more relaxed as he saw Ms. Smith smile and nod during different parts of his informal presentation.

Damian started out slowly. "I think we should use the PA system as a means to address bullying. There could a fifteen-minute segment each day, before classes, that addresses different bullying-related topics. The first day we could give the definition of bullying, followed by a self-assessment to answer the question, are you a bully? The next day, the segment would address the effects of bullying. The third day, it would talk about how to discourage bullying and what to do if you're bullied."

"Damian, I think you have an excellent idea, but whether it gets implemented depends on a review process that requires presentation and approval by the student council and PTA. If you're willing to go through the steps required, I think we can make a difference at Landlin. Thank you again, young man!"

Damian left the office feeling confident and happy. Junior year was turning out to be quite a surprise!

What's for Dinner, Mark?

CHICAGO

ADVENTURE

GREED

KIDNAPPING

SIBLING RIVALRY

What's for Dinner, Mark?

Mark Channing loved to cook. The kitchen was his favorite room in the house. He cooked at work, and when he came home, he cooked to relax. His family loved that. As long as he was around, there was no question that they were going to eat well! The only question was how well. He had started cooking for himself and his brother when both parents were busy working late. His mother would put beans in a slow cooker for him and his brother. There was also usually corn bread batter waiting in the refrigerator. All they had to do was scoop the batter into a muffin tin and bake it.

This ritual started out of necessity when his mother took a second job to help his dad make ends meet. Mark was sixteen at the time, and after a month of eating beans and other slow-cooked meals, he decided something had to give. One day while watching a food channel, Mark saw an advertisement for a cookbook expounding on the virtues of plant-based protein. Most explicitly, all of the recipes were legume-based, or, per Mark's perception, based on beans. Tired of eating slow-cooked beans, he decided to order the cookbook. Within a month, the beans took on a new taste and texture. He was making casseroles, faux meat dishes, etc., all of which tasted nothing like the beans they'd originated from. His aunt, who lived on the floor above them, started conveniently coming down to check on the boys around mealtime.

To help fuel his love for cooking, Mark found a part-time job working, as a short order cook, on weekends and in the evening until he graduated from high school. He wanted to pursue becoming a chef, and so continued to work, as a "short order" cook, at a local greasy spoon. In the evenings he took culinary classes, and worked on new recipes, in his spare time. Most of his relatives thought he was wasting his time and wanted to know, "Boy, what you gonna do with that? You need a real job!" All of Mark's uncles on his dad's side of the family were manual laborers. One worked construction, one was a plumber, and the youngest was an electrician. These were good jobs and for the most part provided a steady income. However, Mark was not excited at the prospect of spending eight to twelve hours a day working on a dusty lot, fixing toilets, or installing wiring. On the other hand, he was inspired by racks of spices, herbs, and flavor extracts. These, coupled with the right cut of meat or custard base, made for time well spent in Mark's view. He was determined to be the best at his craft. His ultimate goal was to own a restaurant with three Michelin stars, and he wanted to be the chef responsible for that rating.

Every other year, the culinary community hosted an open competition for one hundred cooks and would-be chefs. The entries were limited to the first hundred contestants to apply. This wasn't an out-and-out race; anyone who entered had to be ready. It wasn't just about bringing one's A-game, but about the risk that was imminent if one didn't bring their A-game. The judges were selected from among the fiercest food critics around the country. Even those who didn't win wanted to be reviewed favorably. Any slight or negative comment by a judge could ruin their chances of ever becoming a star in the culinary community.

Mark had started preparing six months in advance for this competition. At the age of twenty-four, he decided he was ready. Two years before, after having only been a short order cook for five years and only four years of culinary classes, he didn't think he was ready and didn't want to risk getting a bad review. In the two years since, he had expanded his repertoire of culinary skills, elevated his palate, and gained the patience required to create a great dish. Every day on his break, Mark wrote notes for what was developing into what he thought would be prize winning cuisine. On the weekend, he worked on his entrée by cooking it from beginning to end, tweaking the spices, the cooking time, and the garnishes. When he ran into a problem with the texture or taste of any component, he worked with it until it was perfect. If he couldn't perfect it, he substituted another item. He had done this so often that he was starting to dream about his entrée.

Perfection was dictated by the "Motty Panel," an elite committee consisting of his mom and his pet golden Labrador retriever, Scotty. However, he only allowed Scotty a tablespoon or two of his entrées, as dictated by a list of food ingredients to avoid provided by Scotty's vet. This became a strict rule when Scotty inadvertently developed gastroenteritis after consuming Mark's Quizzee entrée.

He'd taken poor Scotty to the vet. The dog's stomach had to be pumped. After a scolding from Dr. Brown, Mark had been advised to leave Scotty at the hospital overnight. The next day, when he'd gone to check on Scotty, he had found his pet bright-eyed and bushy tailed, jumping up on him and eager to get home.

133

"Now, Mark," the vet had said, "I know how eager pets can be to eat, but you've got to make sure to regulate Scotty's diet. He can have an occasional one or two tablespoons of human food, but nothing on a regular basis."

"Doc, I'm on it!" Mark had replied. He was determined to protect his best friend. So even though Scotty jumped up on the table to get to the human food, Mark still felt at fault. He needed to secure his dishes, but he would make sure not to keep any foods or spices in his home that would be dangerous for Scotty. So he cleaned out his spice pantry and his freezer. From now on he would only cook and use ingredients that were pet-friendly.

After each recipe was perfected, Mark took a serving of the entrée to his mother. If she approved, he placed one or two tablespoons of it in a feeding bowl for Scotty. In another bowl, he placed the dog's favorite moist canned food. Scotty usually sniffed both before he decided which one to eat first. With the last entrée, he sniffed both bowls, ate Mark's creation, and sat in front of the bowl, waiting for more. Mark picked up the gourmet bowl and rinsed it out. Scotty followed him, still hoping for more.

"Oh, no, Mr. Scotty. You need to eat your usual fare." Mark felt guilty about teasing Scotty with a sample of what he hoped would be his winning entrée. He led the shaggy food critic back to the kitchen, to his regular bowl.

Mark was excited about getting his entry ready two months in advance of the opening date. The one flaw was that the complementary sauce needed something more. Ideally, with each bite, the sauce was meant to linger on the palate until the morsel was broken down enough to swallow. Mark decided his options were to either thicken the sauce to keep the flavor from dissipating when it combined with the digestive juices of the mouth, or to adjust the spices to adhere more to the oral lining and extend the flavor's longevity. This, in Mark's perspective, was so that the interplay between the sauce and the meat would be present with each chew until the mouthful was swallowed.

His mother, on the other hand, thought the entrée was perfect. Mark knew that this dish needed to be beyond reproach and felt that his mother was biased because he was her son.

As he dressed to go to work, he closed his small notebook and placed it in his backpack. Whenever he was working on a dish, he dedicated a pocket-sized spiral notebook that he could fit in his apron pocket and write down any ideas that came to him between short orders.

During the course of the day, Mark consulted several culinary references that mentioned numerous ways to enhance various qualities of foods and spices. These were his own personal texts that he had invested in while going to culinary school. It took him the better part of six years to complete what normally would have been a four-year curriculum. That was because he had to work part-time to earn his tuition, but it was well worth it to do what he loved.

Between frying eggs in the morning and flipping burgers in the afternoon, Mark decided that he would first try to thicken the sauce to extend the flavor's time on the palate. Upon driving home, he could hardly wait to get started revising and perfecting the sauce for his entrée. Turning the key in his front door, he was met by Scotty, who knocked him to the floor in his enthusiasm. Deciding that Scotty was hungry, he stopped to feed him before starting his cooking.

With that settled, Mark reached into his backpack to get his spiral notebook. Much to his surprise, it wasn't there. He then recalled the last time he'd had his notebook: he had stuffed it into the side front pocket of his apron while preparing an order for a customer who was in a hurry.

Frantically, Mark rushed back to the Grease Spot, the place where he slung fast food for a livelihood. Rushing past the evening crowd, he sped into the kitchen, looking for the apron he had tossed into the soiled-clothing hamper. He searched all of the aprons, but found no sign of his notebook. Thinking it might have slipped out of the pocket and into the bottom of the hamper, he turned the hamper upside down. Just then, the manager came into the locker room, wondering why Mark had rushed back just after completing his shift.

"Mr. Grey, I left a pocket notebook in the apron I was wearing before I left. I've looked in all the aprons and I can't find it."

"Oh, don't worry, son. It'll turn up. Did you check in the lost and found?" Grey asked.

Mark walked over to a bin where staff placed odds and ends left behind by customers. He found an old keyring and a half-empty package of gum, but no notebook.

He dejectedly left the Grease Spot, knowing that he would probably never see his notebook again. Well, at least he knew the ingredients for his entrée. The more he pondered the disappearance of his notebook, the more he realized he was going to have to start over with a new dish. He couldn't enter a recipe that anyone else might have access to and risk being accused of submitting someone else's work.

The next day, Mark spoke to the waitstaff and the only other cook on duty the previous day to find out if they had happened to see his notebook. But no one admitted to seeing it. He knew someone was lying and he needed to know who the scrub bucket was. He became an amateur sleuth and started observing everyone's behavior throughout his shift. He observed the waitresses who, for the most part, appeared to have no culinary interests. Thom, the other cook, had made no secret of his view that the Grease Spot was just a pit stop on the way to his real career of becoming a writer.

The only other staff he hadn't questioned were the janitors. Gilley had just left on vacation a day ago and probably knew nothing. The other janitor, who was covering for him, didn't appear to be any more aware of the whereabouts of his notebook than anyone else.

Mark decided to set a trap. The next day he left another spiral notebook in his apron, dusted with itching powder that was part of a gag gift he had received several years before, but never thought he would have any use for. If anyone took his notebook, they would spend most of the workday scratching. There would be no reward in taking this book since the recipe it contained was for a basic omelet.

The next day, Mark arrived at work, excited by the prospect of one of his coworkers exhibiting symptoms of pruritus—itching. However, when he went back to the place where he'd left the apron, it was still there with the spiral notebook. He left the apron in place for another day. When he came in the second day, no one had taken the bait.

"Hey, Mark, that apron has been on the rack for two days. You need to put it in the dirty linen hamper. You should have done that when you changed aprons two days ago."

"Not a problem, Mr. Grey."

Mark gave up on this plan, but was determined to find out who the culprit was.

The next week, Gilley was back from vacation, and since he was the only person Mark hadn't asked about his spiral notebook, Mark approached him when he came in on the evening shift to clean up.

"Hey how was your vacation?"

"Good, great, wonderful . . . but too short!"

"Good to hear! Let me ask you a question. Before you left for vacation, did you come across a spiral notebook with a recipe in it? It was in my apron on a wall hook."

"Nah, man, I didn't. Wish I could help you. But if I see it, I'll let you know!"

He sounded convincing. But, thus far, no one knew anything. There was no clue as to what happened to his spiral notebook.

Over the next two months, Mark worked diligently at creating a new dish and contest entry. However, he still had an uneasiness about the people he worked with, feeling that he could no longer trust them.

Approximately a week before the contest was scheduled to open, he had perfected his new dish. It was Motty approved; both his mom and Scotty had passed it with flying colors. Scotty, after receiving two tablespoons of the new dish, refused to eat his favorite canned dog food. Finally, after several hours, he returned to it reluctantly. Mark learned his lesson and would never exceed the limits Scotty's doctor had placed on the amount of human food he could have at any given time. Also, the hospital bill for Scotty's prior misadventure with human food discouraged Mark from letting it happen again.

Finally the website for the contest was up, and it listed the rules and details of how the contest worked. Mark had read the rules in prior years and could recite them even if he were awakened from a deep sleep at midnight.

So when his mom asked him about the contest, he was able to give her more details than she cared to know. They had been talking casually about his work and future plans when he told her about the Master Three Culinary Cup.

"I'm so excited. I believe I have a chance to win this year."

"Do you think your stolen recipe could have anything to do with the contest?" his mother postulated.

"I don't think so. No one at the Grease Spot seems to have an interest in food beyond the everyday activity of the restaurant."

"Mark, how did you come to find out about the contest?"

"Well, Mom, it's almost like a well-kept secret that's hiding in plain sight. I discovered it about ten years ago when I was searching on the web for something . . . I can't remember what. But, at any rate, after reading the details, I was determined to enter it one day. It's like the Grand Prix of the culinary society. There are several steps to go through.

"Every two years, a pop-up website site for the Master Three Culinary Cup appears. It's up for thirty days as a promotion. On the thirty-first day, it officially allows entries. The first one hundred recipes are automatically the official contestants. Each entrant is given a registration number that allows them to follow their progress throughout the contest."

"So, the first entrants aren't necessarily the best, but the quickest? That seems a little unfair. Don't you think, Mark?"

"I guess. But it also selects those who are the most motivated since only a hundred participants are allowed! Then, from there, seventy-five entrants are dropped just by a review of the recipes."

"Who makes that decision?"

Mark was delighted that his mom was showing a real interest in how the contest worked. "Not just anyone. Twelve renowned chefs take ten days to select the twenty-five best recipes. The results are posted online."

"Can you enter anything? Like, could I enter Aunt Emma's praline pie?"

"The rules stipulate that the recipe must be original and consist of all fresh ingredients. During any given contest year, the recipe category might be entrées, appetizers, or desserts. This contest year, the category is entrées. Which is good for me, since that's where I excel.

"The top twenty-five recipes will then be prepared, by the panel of chef's, and served to twelve of the world's most famous food critics. From this group, ten finalists will be selected. This process takes twenty days, and the results are available online. If you're in the top ten, you are invited to the final presentation of the Master Three Culinary Cup. The last ten dishes will be placed on the menu of an unnamed restaurant somewhere in the US. The contest entries will be listed at random. At the end of another thirty days, the entrée with the most orders wins. The winner will be announced at the awards dinner, where the first-place entrée will be served as part of a four-course meal."

"Wow, Mark. That's impressive. I hope the prize is well worth the trouble!"

"It is, Mom. You get to train at a famous restaurant in Paris with a world-famous chef, Francois Latrec. In the past twenty-two years of its existence, no one from Chicago has ever won. I'm determined to be the first."

On March 31, Mark went to bed early to make sure that he awakened at 11:45 p.m. He wanted to be sitting at his computer, poised to obtain one of the one hundred coveted slots for the Master Three Culinary Cup. Other chefs had told him these slots could fill up within minutes, so Mark was determined not to lose out on this opportunity due to chance.

On April 1 at 12:01 a.m., Mark had arrived at the official website, and within two or three minutes he had registered and uploaded his recipe. He wrote down his registration number and placed it in his file cabinet, where he kept all of his important documents.

Over the next ten days, Mark went from feeling very confident to questioning whether he should have even entered the contest. He didn't tell any of his friends that he had entered and, true to form, if any of them had entered, they weren't telling. Anyone who was going to be eliminated from the contest wanted to be among the first seventy-five. If he made it to the food critic phase, he could be slammed with a bad review that could show up later on in his culinary career.

That day, Mark was in a really good mood. A casual friend of his came in for breakfast with his parents. It was a Saturday ritual that they had been doing for as long as Mark had been working at the Grease Spot.

"Hey, Mark." Morry waved to him from the table where they were sitting. Mark had just gotten started and was putting on his apron.

"Y'all gonna have the usual?"

"You bet!"

"Well, I'll get started while Marie formally takes your order." Mark started preparing the corn bread that Morry and the Allens loved.

"You're in a really good mood. Did you win the lotto or something?" Morry teased.

"Nah, man! But I can dream!" Mark wanted to tell someone other than his mother about the contest, but decided against it. If he didn't make a decent showing, he didn't want to have to discuss it with anyone.

On April 11, Mark went home and fed Scotty as usual. He looked at his computer with apprehension, anxiety, and excitement. He wanted to know if he had made it through the first phase, but wondered how he would feel if he hadn't. As he prepared to log in to the Master Three Culinary Cup website, Scotty came and sat at his feet. Scotty didn't hang around when Mark worked on his computer because there was little attention to be had from his master at these times. However, Scotty could sense that there was something different about this computer session, so he nestled up beside Mark's feet, slowly wagging his tail. Mark went to the website. His mouth was dry and his hands were sweating. Carefully, logging in with the assigned registration number, Mark held his breath.

After the last digit, the screen lit up with confetti and streamers. Mark jumped up. "Booyah! That's what I'm talking about!" Scotty joined in the excitement, barking and running after Mark as he did his happy dance. Mark was officially in the top twenty-five contestants and was going on to the second phase. He knew at this point that he was all in and subject to full review once the critics tasted his fare.

* * * * * * *

On May 1, Mark was anxious to get home to find out if he had progressed to phase two. He could have logged in to the website before going to work, but decided against it since he was in a really good mood and didn't want to ruin it in the event he had been eliminated.

This time, he was less anxious but still had nervous energy, that Scotty once again sensed. However, Scotty stood up, poised to run with Mark if he broke out into his happy dance again. Scotty wanted to keep up since the last time

Mark did the happy dance, he got two extra treats outside of mealtime.

Mark logged in to the website. This time, there was no instant gratification. He would have to go through the list of registration numbers to find out if he was in the top ten. He couldn't decide whether to start from the top or the bottom of the list. He wondered if it would be better to be eliminated before getting his hopes up too high, or to start from the top and have his hopes dashed after not finding his number by the time he reached the bottom.

Mark decided to start from the top. By the time he got to number five, he didn't see his registration. He was beginning to wonder if starting from the bottom may have been better. Now he was checking the numbers more slowly and intently, not wanting to miss his number if he had indeed made it to the third phase. By the time, he reached the eighth entry, he saw his registration number, as clear as day. He breathed a sigh of relief. There was no happy dance. Instead, there was a silent prayer of gratitude. Scotty still got extra treats and an extra walk since Mark wanted to get out of his condo and run off the nervous energy that had built up during the course of the day. Scotty enjoyed getting to go out twice that day and began to feel as if the flat, thin box on the table was his good luck charm. He would have to pay more attention to this thing that was getting him extra treats and fresh air.

* * * * * * *

From May 2 to May 9, preparation was being made for the ten finalists to enter phase three, which involved public scrutiny. The chef panel had made the first cut of the entrants, the food critics had had their say, and now the public would weigh in. However, the public wouldn't know they were judging a contest. The entrées would be randomly placed on the menu at a four- or five-star restaurant, along with the usual items. They would all be priced equally so as not to introduce any bias based on price. The quantity of food would be the same. At the end of thirty days, the entrée with the most orders would win. The tally would be automated based on computer data and submitted to an accounting firm for review and confirmation of the winner.

The winner would be announced at an awards dinner on June 13 at Chez Charrise, a local five-star restaurant in Chicago. Mark was happy about this since he didn't enjoy the preparation involved in traveling and going through airport security. He was also happy because Chez Charrise was known for its food and for attracting multiple local and international celebrities. He had once caught a glimpse of Dr. Jonathan Stein leaving Chez Charrise. Mark remembered him from the cover of *a science based* magazine some years ago, in which he'd been featured for an invention of some sort. Mark really couldn't remember the invention since science wasn't his thing.

As June 13 approached, Mark was ready. He had invited his parents as two of his plus-three guests. He actually wanted to get Scotty a tux, and have him as the third guest. However, he was pretty sure animals weren't invited, and with all the food that was going to be on display, any animal presence would lead to pandemonium. He quickly decided his aunt would be a good substitute. He remembered from his earlier years that she would often come downstairs to check on him and his brother, conveniently at mealtime, when his parents worked late. It was during these years that Mark started honing his culinary skills. His brother, who was away at med school, wished him luck and told him he would be there in spirit.

The evening of June 13, Mark and his guests arrived at 6:00 p.m. It was requested that the finalists and their guests arrive an hour early in order to be seated and to get instructions for the evening's program. The event was open to the public via advance ticket sales, from one hundred to three hundred dollars a seat and priced based on the vicinity to the stage. All the contestants and their guests were in the first row of tables. The table settings were luxurious, beyond anything Mark had ever experienced. Maybe he had seen exquisite settings in culinary magazines, but he had never been up close and personal with settings that he would have the pleasure of using.

The emcee for the evening was Francois Latrec, owner and master chef of Le Prix, a three-star Michelin rated restaurant in Paris. The winner of the contest would win three hundred thousand dollars and a six-month internship with Francois. Mark already knew that if he won, he would use the prize money to help get his culinary skills cookbook published. The book contained not only recipes, but tips for elevating one's cooking skills. Maybe not as a master chef, because he wasn't quite there yet, but at least a junior chef.

As the waitstaff served the appetizers and then the salad, everyone was trying to guess whether his or her entrée was the winner since all other courses of a meal have to complement the entrée.

Right before the entrée was served, Francois came to the stage to make a special announcement.

"Attention! Attention, everyone! We have an unprecedented predicament. We have a tie! I have consulted our panel of master chefs. We have decided that in order to break the tie, we will have the top two contestants sample the other's dish. Afterward, they are to guess as many ingredients of the other contestant's dish as possible. The one who guesses the most ingredients accurately will be the winner. Our top two contestants are Mr. Mark Channing and Mr. Gordon Gilbert. Mr. Channing and Mr. Gilbert, please come to the stage."

Gordon Gilbert was Gilley, the janitor at the Grease Spot. Mark's thoughts were racing. How was the janitor one of the top two contestants in a cooking contest? Gordon Gilbert looked nervous as he caught a glimpse of Mark's dumbfounded look.

Mark was speechless as they were both taken to separate rooms for the unprecedented fourth phase of the contest. The dish that was set in front of Mark had a very familiar aroma and appearance.

Mark decided to withhold final judgement until he actually tasted the dish. Sure enough, with the first forkful of food, Mark recognized the signature dish that he had been working on when he left his spiral notebook at the restaurant. He angrily wrote down all the ingredients that he knew were part of the entrée Gilley had submitted. He thought about how to expose Gordon Gilbert for the fraud that he was. Mark couldn't prove this was his recipe, but he was determined not to let this perpetrator get away with submitting Mark's work as his own.

Ten minutes later, the monitors came and took Mark's list of ingredients from Gilley's entrée. Likewise, the list was collected from Gilley. Mark and Gordon were allowed to return to their seats while the lists were reviewed.

Upon Mark's return to his seat, his mother was puzzled. "Mark, what's wrong? You look like you've seen a ghost!"

Mark knew that he would have to wait until later to explain to his parents what had transpired.

Just then, Francois returned to the stage. "Ladies, gentlemen, and chefs, the twenty-third winner of the Master Three Culinary Cup contest is Mr. Mark Channing. What a remarkable palate! He identified every single ingredient in Mr. Gordon's recipe. Come on up, Mark!"

Mark jumped up and walked to the stage, his exhilaration tempered by his anger at Gilley.

"Well done!" Francois stated as he handed Mark the gold-plated oversized cup that would later be engraved with Mark's name, the year, and the location of the Master Three Culinary Cup contest.

Mark managed to smile broadly, scanning the room to catch a glimpse of the object of his wrath. Just as Gordon was looking around for a convenient exit, Francois invited him to come up as well. Gordon walked slowly to the stage, not wanting to be in the same room with the man whose work he had presented as his own.

Gordon leaned forward to shake Mark's hand. Mark leaned in at the same instant and told Gordon that they needed to talk. As they walked off the stage, Mark was close on Gordon's heels although the thief was trying to run. Just then, Mark grabbed Gordon by the back of his collar. Pausing in the hallway, fifteen feet from the stage, Gilley began to confess.

"Okay, okay, I'm not going anywhere. I know you're angry and I can explain. I've always had an interest in cooking. I thought if I got a job at a restaurant, I could eventually work my way up to being a cook, and advance from there. So when I

148

was cleaning up at the Spot months ago and found your spiral notebook as I was placing the aprons in the dirty linen hamper, I thought it was a sign. I took the recipe and cooked it at home. Man, it was the best thing I've ever tasted! So I decided to enter the contest. I never dreamed that the recipe was yours or that you would be entering this contest."

"First, Gilley, how do you even know about this contest, let alone think you could win it?"

"I not only aspire to be a chef, but also read the culinary magazines, which had the contest information listed. Since I'm unable to afford culinary school, I figured if I won, I could get on-the-job training to advance my cause."

"Well, for one thing, Gilley, even now, the fact that you came in second in a major culinary contest is going to open doors for you. However, your peers and future employers are going to assume you have certain basic culinary skills, and when they find out you don't, the doors are going to close just as quickly as they opened. So you've actually sabotaged your culinary career before it's gotten started."

"So, what now? Are you going to turn me in?"

"I have no evidence. You do need to be punished, but just knowing that taking what you thought was a shortcut is going to be your downfall is enough for me!"

Mark turned his back and walked away, content to know that his family was proud of him and Scotty was waiting at home to be walked. What a life, and he was living it. Six months in Paris! Wow!

CHICAGO

ADVENTURE

GREED

KIDNAPPING

SIBLING RIVALRY

The Fabulous Frederico

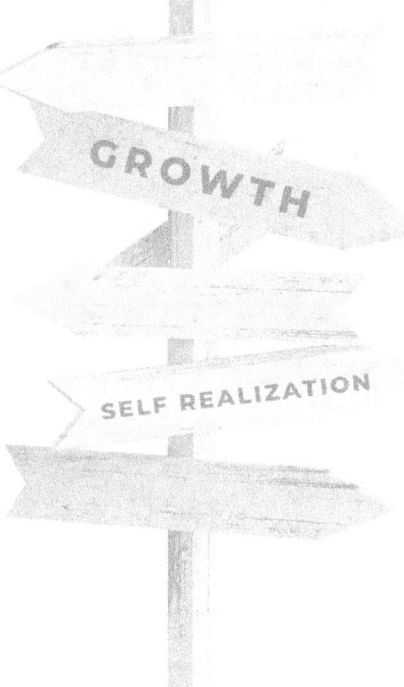

CHICAGO

ADVENTURE

GREED

KIDNAPPING

SIBLING RIVALRY

The Fabulous Frederico

Morrison Allen groaned as he turned on his side, cushioned only by a grocery cardboard box split at the seams to lay flat. The coldness of the pavement radiated upward and caused him to shudder as he awakened from an almost sleepless night. Living on the street for several years, after living in his car for five years, had taken its toll. He felt much older than his chronological forty-plus years. He had left medical school in his third year, but actually knew in the second year that medicine was not what he wanted to spend the rest of his life doing.

He had talked with his mother about it and she had emphatically stated, "Morry, honey, it's only two more years. Once you are done with training and are your own boss, you will love it!"

So he toughed it out, and by his third year, he was a hundred degrees past fried. It had been trying just to get to class. Once there, he'd had problems paying attention long enough to take notes. Memorizing the Krebs cycle or other minutiae absolutely left him feeling in the dumps. What made it worse was that his parents were absolutely ecstatic at the prospect of having a doctor in the family.

Morry was an artist at heart. When he was in high school, his art teacher had promised that she could get him a four-year scholarship to college if he majored in art. He'd been so excited, he could hardly wait to tell his parents.

His dad was a postal worker and his mother was a housewife. Although they had been saving for his college training, this would take care of that issue. He was always an exceptional student and had been in the National Honor Society, so he'd felt he would be able to get some scholastic scholarships, too. He had also known that he could still try to get into medical school, if he wanted to, by completing all the required courses and taking the MCAT.

But by that point, he wasn't sure if he still wanted to pursue a medical career. A lot had happened since he'd declared at seven years old that he wanted to be a doctor. However, whenever he'd mentioned the possibility of doing something else, his mother had always reminded him of it. However, at seven, there were a lot of things he wanted to be: a lawyer, teacher, designer, male model, etc. He had just happened to mention being a doctor, and now he was being held to something he'd mentioned in passing. Wanting to please his parents, Morry felt trapped.

One day while in gross anatomy class, Morry had grown tired of the smell of formaldehyde and of being surrounded by overeager medical students rushing to dissect out all ten structures needed to be able to leave the lab after a two-hour session. He had usually been the one who did most of the work of dissection, in his four member anatomy group. One student stood around with a fan that he brought to each session to dissipate the smell. The other two stood there gossiping about who had failed the last midterm and who was flunking out.

This was when Morry had put down his scalpel and blunt probe, loaded up his instruments, and walked out.

"Hey, man, where you going? We've only identified three structures!"

"You mean *I've* identified three structures. I'm done!" Morry had responded to one of the gossiping members of his team.

"Well, see you in biochem tomorrow."

Not if I can help it, he'd thought.

He had promptly emptied his locker, gone to the dean's office, and officially resigned.

Gross anatomy then had consisted of dissecting cadavers to identify organs and other soft-tissue structures and then labeling them. This method helped familiarize the medical student with the human body. It had been Morry's least favorite class and the tipping point of finally acting on his decision to quit medical school.

He had arrived home feeling lighter than he had in the previous two years and some months. He'd then decided to kick back and veg out in front of his TV for several hours. Too tired to eat, he had gone to bed early, at 8:00 p.m.

Morry needed to tell his parents that he had spent two years of his life doing something he absolutely hated and had no intention of returning to it. The next day was Saturday, and he would tell them when they met for breakfast, something they'd done every two weeks just to keep in touch. At twenty-two years old, Morry should have been free to pursue his own future, but he'd dreaded facing his parents after four years of college tuition and other expenses that they had footed. They'd told him he didn't need to pay them back, but that was when they'd still thought they were going to have a doctor in the family.

That early September morning, the air had been crisp, with a freshness reminiscent of biting into a tart, crunchy McIntosh apple, cleansing the taste buds. The leaves had just started to turn, and Morry had found himself thinking back to the many other September mornings he'd met his parents for breakfast. This was the first time he hadn't looked forward to it.

At 8:00 a.m., he'd gotten into his twelve-year-old hooptie and headed down Fifty-Fifth Street toward Hyde Park Boulevard. They'd planned to meet at the Grease Spot. It was a little hole-in-the-wall restaurant with the best stone-ground grits, homemade sausage, melt-in-your-mouth corn bread, and a myriad of other dishes not readily found at other restaurants. Morry loved the corn bread that was made from a seven-grain batter, with only one-seventh of its content from cornmeal. The other grains were a secret, as was the ingredient that kept the bread moist and tasty. Morry had planned to have his usual corn bread with sausage and a made-to-order omelet. These delights would be accompanied by freshly squeezed grapefruit juice and fresh ground coffee.

He'd been acquainted with some of the staff, but his favorite cook had always been Mark Channing. They were close to the same age, and Mark had confided in him about becoming a world-class chef. Mark had likewise encouraged Morry to follow his dreams of becoming an artist.

Upon his arrival at 8:30 a.m., Mr. and Mrs. Allen, the proud parents of the future Dr. Allen, had been sitting at a corner table, waiting patiently. As Morry had crossed the room, his mouth had become as dry as cotton.

"Hi, son! How's it going?" Morry's dad and mom had stood up together to give him a group hug.

"Hey, Mom! Hey Dad! I'm doing well," Morry had lied. Every minute he'd spent in medical school had been a never-ending nightmare.

Eighteen plus years had passed since then, so the details of the rest of the conversation, he couldn't recall. What he did recall was how hurt they were. He believed his mother had even cried, and he recalled the culmination of the conversation, when his Dad had insisted that he was throwing his life away.

The Saturday breakfasts had continued, but were a little strained. The tension had started to ease once Morry pursued being a realtor. He'd obtained his license, and things had gone well until the 2008 housing crash. Because Morry had overextended himself, he had no real savings to sustain him during the lean times, but continued to try to make a go of it. He downsized bit by bit until there was nothing left to downsize. He'd gone from a lavish Gold Coast penthouse condominium to a small old-town apartment, then a studio apartment, and then finally to his car. His parents had invited him to move back home, but there was no way he was doing that. He didn't want to be that guy who would have to face the disappointment of moving back home. He also didn't want to see his mom shake her head when she thought he wasn't looking, sneaking sideway glances at her husband. It was bad enough to go through this every two weeks when they met for breakfast.

After selling his car, he'd had to start living on the street. This should have compelled him to consider moving back home, but Morry was too proud. He had lost everything, but still hadn't pursued his dream of painting. He felt as if his life was moving in reverse.

So when he awakened that cold November morning, Morry was starting to rethink his options.

Looking in his panhandler's cup, he saw a measly five dollars and change. After removing the five loose dollars, Morry was surprised to see a lotto ticket at the bottom of the cup. The drawing hadn't taken place, but was scheduled for the following night. Morry wondered who would drop a lotto ticket into a panhandler's cup. The drawing had reached a record high of $380 million. He eagerly signed his name on the back of the ticket and dreamed of the possibilities of independence that would come with such a large sum of money. But he knew the odds were against him.

Morry started his day with a new perspective; he really didn't think he would win, but what if this was an indication that his luck was about to change? Gathering up his belongings and cart, Morry went to the local gas station, where he was able to attempt to wash up. Normally only customers could use the bathroom, but the owner had taken a liking to Morry, who reminded him of a brother who had passed away several years before. He wanted to help Morry and even offered him a job. Morry decided against this since he was determined that his getting off the street this time would have to be predicated on him making progress toward pursuing his dream.

Morry still had his pride, so he always bought something at the gas station. Sometimes it was a sandwich or a package of gum, depending on how much he was able to panhandle from the day before. This day he put his backpack down to look for a few coins to buy a package of gum.

Just as the backpack touched the floor, Morry saw a dirty, round mound of fur come from nowhere. In a flash, the creature sped around the corner with the blue backpack, dragging it on the ground.

"Hey, hey, hey! Come back here, you mutt!" Morry assumed what he saw was a dog, but the animal was so fast, he wasn't sure. Also the rancid odor that trailed behind the dog, was like a mixture of garlic, onions, and some other fetid odor. Maybe it was a rat.

Morry flew after, what he assumed was a dog, but lost sight of it when it ducked into the alley, through a gangway, and under a house. Morry had dragged his cart along with him, so he wasn't able to move very fast. At the moment he lost sight of the stray, he remembered that the lotto ticket was in the side pocket of the backpack.

Morry was devastated. That ticket could be worth millions—or not. Morry would never know without the ticket in hand. He decided to see if he could get a line on the mutt, which was obviously homeless, like himself. He went to Washington Park, where he spent most of his days, just to get fresh air. That dirty little ball of fur looked familiar. Morry then remembered seeing a poster of a similar snowy white Pomeranian that was missing. There was a reward of a thousand dollars since the dog was described as a show dog. The owners thought the dog had been stolen because it was pedigreed and bred for show.

Morry decided he would try to catch the dog and collect the reward, if indeed this was the same dog below all that filth. While he was trying to figure out a plan, Ben came and sat down on the park bench next to him.

"Hey, man, how you doing? You look like you're in deep thought." Ben was the closest thing to a friend that Morry could claim since living on the street. Ben was only partially homeless. Once the temperature dropped below freezing, he moved indoors, living with his sister during the winters. She really wanted him to stop living on the street completely and had offered him her spare bedroom to entice him. However, Ben loved the freedom of coming and going without any ties to anyone or any responsibility. He was a snowbird of the homeless sort, a fair-weather bum. His clothes were clean and he was able to do laundry and bathe at his sister's at least once a week, even while on the street. This made him an aristocrat among the homeless community.

"Yes, I just got ripped off by a mutt that ran off with my backpack."

"Oh, well, you can kiss it goodbye. If he didn't bury it, he probably ripped it up so bad, it's going to be useless."

Morry debated whether he should tell Ben about the lotto ticket. "Well, there's a reward for the dog. You remember the posters for the white Pomeranian?'

"Yeah, but those posters haven't been up for a while. How would you find out who to return the dog to? Also, usually dogs that valuable have a chip. They should have found him by now."

"Well, what if they haven't?" Morry countered.

"You can check at the local post office to see if they have any posters."

"Maybe you could check for me. You're more presentable; even though I've washed up at the gas station, I still look shabby."

Ben was sixty-two years old, with graying temples that gave him a distinguished look. He also had a refinement that would never belie his lack of an address.

"How much was the reward?" Ben had to decide if it was worth taking the time to walk to the local post office. After all, he valued his leisure time of doing nothing in particular and everything in general. The latter consisted of sitting on a park bench, people-watching. Ben had stopped working at the age of fifty. He hadn't really retired, per se, since he didn't have a pension or retirement funds. He'd just decided he had spent enough time punching a clock and refused to do it anymore.

"If I remember correctly, it's a grand!"

"Well, let's get going!" Suddenly Ben had newfound energy and headed toward the post office.

"I'll come, too, and wait outside." Morry was on Ben's heels. Once inside, Ben looked around on the bulletin board that contained the "wanted" posters, etc. There was nothing about missing pets on the board.

"Can I help you?" the postal clerk queried Ben.

"Yes, miss, I'm looking for the missing pet posters."

"That board is around the corner, near the P.O. boxes."

As Ben approached the designated area, the poster of the Pomeranian stood out. The dog was strikingly beautiful, with the whitest, fluffiest fur that Ben had ever seen. He had noticed the poster before, on the street, but hadn't paid much attention to it. He took it down and went to the counter to see if he could get a copy of it.

"Oh, you can have that. We were getting ready to discard it; the owner is no longer offering the reward."

"Do you know why? Because my friend believes he's seen this dog on the street."

"I'm not sure. But there's a phone number on the poster that you can use to contact the owner."

When he spotted his friend leaving the post office, Morry raced up to Ben, almost knocking him over. "What did you find out?"

"Well, there's no longer a reward, but if you still want to try to rescue your backpack, we can call the owner to see if they have some additional info that might help us track down this fleabag.

"Here on the poster, it states the dog's name is Frederico. Fleabag Fred—how about that nickname for a runaway dog?"

Ben handed the phone to Morry and read the number off of the poster aloud while Morry dialed.

"Hello," a hesitant voice answered. "Can I help you?"

"Yes, my name is Morry Allen. I'm calling about your missing dog. He grabbed my backpack while I was at the local gas station, and I'm trying to find him to get it back. So if you could maybe give me some clues about where I might find him, I would appreciate it!"

"Hi, Mr. Allen. Now, just so you know, there's no longer a reward for him. He stays on the street, which is where he wants to be."

"Why don't you want him back?"

"It's not that we don't want him; he doesn't want to be here with us." The owner went on to explain. "The first time Frederico went missing, we thought someone had dognapped him out of the backyard. After all, he is a pedigreed dog. So when he was found and brought back, we were thrilled. I gladly paid the one grand. A few weeks later, he was in the backyard with my son and daughter. They were playing fetch. Corey threw the ball for Fred to retrieve it. Fred ran past the ball, and with the running start he had, he jumped over the fence.

"That's when I knew he had most likely run away the first time. Now, to answer your second question, Fred is a creature of habit and loves food. He has been seen hanging out at Handler's Grocery and Grill, especially on Thursdays, when they clean out their storage pantry and freezer.

"So you may be able to catch up with him there, but how that's going to help you get your backpack returned, I don't know. He's probably discarded it in an alley, torn it up, or buried it like a bone."

"How did you come to own Fred?"

"We bought him as a therapeutic pet for my son, Corey. Dr. Blake, our family psychiatrist, recommended getting a pet for Corey to draw him out because of his autism. Corey loved that dog. He petted the dog so much, Fred developed pressure sores. My daughter fell in love with Fred as well. She would dress him in her old baby clothes to have tea parties with her friends."

The owner continued. "I had great plans for that dog. I enrolled him in obedience school. I was grooming him to become a show dog. You see, he had it all, and that ingrate ran away!"

"I hope that helps, but unless there's gold in that backpack, I would forget it and buy another one."

"Whew! Thanks for the info." Morry took a deep breath, thinking that this was way more information than he needed to know.

When Morry hung up, Ben let out a hearty laugh. He was barely able to contain himself until Morry was off the phone. "That dog was traumatized. No wonder he ran away. He had more jobs than some people!" Morry had put the owner on speakerphone so Ben could listen and help out with the search.

"Well, I don't know about you, but I'm hungry. Let's go back to the food kitchen," Ben said, heading down Fifty-Ninth Street.

After eating half of the contents of the lunch box, including a turkey sandwich on rye, bean salad, bottled juice, chocolate chip cookies, and chocolate milk, Morry went to Handler's.

It wasn't delivery day, but he thought he might still catch a glimpse of Fred waiting for handouts.

Crossing at the corner, Morry saw a beer delivery truck pull up opposite Handler's. The driver was making a delivery to the liquor store on the corner. As Morry stepped off of the curb, a dark mass that looked like a mop ran from under a car, crossing the path of the delivery guy, who had started to unload cases of beer. He fell and dropped a case, and the bottles crashed.

"Why, you dirty little...". The man continued to curse at Fred as he picked himself up from the ground. In the meantime, Fred circled around the back side of the truck and crept back up to the puddle of beer, licking up as much as he could until the driver swatted him away.

Morry assumed that, depending on how much beer Fred had consumed, he wouldn't survive the night. He wasn't sure where he had learned this information, but he did recall that alcohol was toxic to dogs.

Fred had been sleeping under the car for warmth when he awakened to a familiar scent, the same scent as the backpack he had swiped earlier that day. Thinking that Morry had found him, Fred darted from under the car to get away from Morry as he crossed the street in the direction of the beer trunk. Morry was totally unaware of Fred's presence, under the car.

Morry wanted to laugh, but thought better of it since the driver was totally upset by this series of events.

"They need to get that worthless, two-bit fleabag, dirty little monster, off the street," the delivery guy continued until he had run out of adjectives and descriptives.

165

The onlookers, who up until then were going about their daily tasks, agreed.

"Yeah, just the other day, I was on my way home and I saw the mutt tearing out of Schultz's Bakery. His mouth was covered with white frosting. At the time I didn't know that's what it was. I thought he had rabies. I found out later that he had knocked down a display of cupcakes and was frantically devouring them when he was chased out of the store!"

Someone else chimed in. "He's a health hazard to our kids. What if he bites someone? He looks as if he has every bacteria and virus known to man and animals."

"Yeah, he's so awful, even his owner doesn't want him back!" The insults went on and on.

After about five minutes of Fred-bashing, Morry had heard enough. He went back to the park, two blocks away, to eat the rest of his lunch. Sitting on his favorite bench, he picked up a discarded newspaper from the day before. He was about ready to bite into the other half of his sandwich when he heard a low-pitched growl, accompanied by a most foul odor. Lowering the newspaper, he saw a dirty pile of fur, barking and baring its teeth.

There stood Fred in all of his filth. At this moment, Morry didn't really know if he still wanted the backpack. The risk of infection might outweigh the benefits since he didn't have health insurance. It would only be worth it if the lotto ticket was a winner . . . and what were the odds? But even more amazing to Morry was that Fred hadn't succumbed to the alcohol. Man this must be some dog!!

"Here's the little gangster of the canine pack, still running free." Morry spoke to Fred in a low, soothing tone as he tossed pieces of the sandwich toward Fred, who stood outside of striking distance.

Fred stopped growling long enough to snatch up and gulp down the bits of bread and meat. Morry was careful not to provoke Fred, who was also under the influence of beer. He thought the dog might indeed be drunk since he had the audacity to track Morry and confront him. After the sandwich was gone, Fred slowly retreated and ran up the street into the darkness. It was now well past 5:00 p.m. Morry knew it was also time for him to get back to his place in the park, where Ben had reserved a sleeping spot under an overpass. Earlier in the day, Morry had left his cart with Ben, who agreed to watch it while he went to Handler's to see if he could catch a sighting of Fred.

They took turns finding places to sleep in the park. For the past week, they had found a dry area where other homeless individuals were quick to reserve places, so Ben had headed there immediately after lunch.

As he walked under the overpass, he could see Ben working a crossword puzzle with a small pocket light. No doubt this was something his sister had given him, as one of the items that would be of convenience while living on the street.

"Hey, how did it work out? Did you see Old Fleabag?" Ben was quite amused by the backstory of Fred's life on the lam.

"Yeah, actually, I saw him twice! He was indeed hanging around Handler's as his owner predicted. While there, he caused some havoc by tripping the beer delivery guy when he ran across his path. The guy dropped a case of bottles, leaving a puddle of beer on the street. Fred lapped up as much as he could. Man, it was so skilled, I couldn't tell if maybe Fred had planned it. Then, while I was sitting on the park bench, he confronted me with growling and posturing, like he wanted to attack me. By then, I just felt sorry for him and ended up giving him the rest of my sandwich."

"Sounds like Fred has street cred. He was able to get beer and a sandwich today and didn't put in any time at a job. That's a dog after my own heart!" Ben laughed. "Are you still going to try to get your backpack?"

"I don't know. I can probably get another government phone and colored pencils. You know I don't want the toothbrush since I wouldn't put anything in my mouth from the pack at this point." While living on the street, Morry had continued to sketch using a paper pad and colored pencils that he purchased with money from panhandling.

Morry still hadn't told Ben about the ticket and decided to hold off on it since he didn't know if he wanted to pursue it any further. Ben was a good friend and Morry would miss him when he went to live with his sister in the coming weeks. At the same time, he wasn't sure he would consider giving Ben half of his lotto winnings if he hit the jackpot.

Over the next week, Morry continued to go to the same park bench every day. It had become sort of a ritual. Fred would show up about the same time, and Morry would give him the remains of his box lunch. Fred continued to keep his distance, growling as if to warn Morry not to do anything rash. On the fourth visit, Fred stopped growling and actually wagged his tail as Morry spoke to him in a calming voice.

"Look here, you little scum bucket, you have something of mine. I'm tired of playing nice. There are people out there who have it in for you, so you better watch your back. I'm your friend, but not for long if I don't get my backpack back!" It was the sound of Morry's voice that Fred responded to, and not the words, since they were less than flattering.

So Fred continued to return. On the seventh day, Fred showed up as usual. After eating Morry's leftovers, he walked away a few feet, then came back to Morry, wagging his tail. Morry wasn't sure what else Fred wanted.

"Food's all gone." He showed Fred the empty box. Fred ran a few feet, then returned, wagging his tail and barking. This bark was not hostile or aggressive. Morry finally understood that Fred wanted him to follow.

Morry followed Fred from about ten feet back, trying to avoid smelling the stench of doggy street life. He hadn't been aware of the intensity of the odor before since Fred always kept a safe distance when Morry fed him.

After about three blocks, Fred ran up under a porch and disappeared. Morry wasn't sure if they were playing a game, or what. About three minutes later, Fred returned with fresh dirt on his paws and a dirty white sweater hanging in his mouth. Triumphantly, he dropped the sweater at Morry's feet. Morry looked perturbed. Fred looked up at Morry, wondering why he didn't appear pleased.

"Oh, you think this is mine?" Morry shook his head. Fred dragged the sweater back to the hole it had come out of and quickly but effectively covered it in dirt again.

Several blocks later, the same process occurred, and this time Fred brought back a Raggedy Ann doll. Morry looked at it, thinking, now if this was cleaned up, it might be something of value for a garage sale or antique sale, just due to the nostalgia. Raggedy Ann dolls had been popular in the 1950s. Morry hesitated for only a minute, shaking his head in the negative, before Fred returned the doll to its hole.

At this point, Morry was tired and knew he needed to get back to the underpass to relieve Ben from saving his place. "Okay, Fred, time to call it a day." He turned to walk in the opposite direction. Before he left, Fred ran up beside him and sniffed him again for really good measure.

Morry wasn't sure why, but he humored Fred by not pulling away, which was his initial instinct.

When Morry arrived at the underpass, Ben had news for him. "Hey, Morry, whatever you plan to do about Fred and your backpack, you better do it soon! I went to the post office today to rent a P.O. box with some money my sister gave me, and there's a new poster for Fred. But it's not for return to his owner. It's from the Humane Society. They want to get Fred off the street, and they're offering a hundred dollars to anyone who turns him in. Odds are they'll be able to catch him on their own, but just for good measure, this is an incentive for reporting his whereabouts. Also, once they capture him, if no one claims him, they'll euthanize him."

"Honestly, I don't know what to do. Fred dug up some junk today and presented it to me, but of course none of it was mine. He may not even know where the backpack is, or that it's mine."

The next day, Morry went to the park bench at 1:00 p.m., the usual time of his "Fred meetings."

A few minutes later, Fred appeared, but this time he trotted up with Morry's backpack in his mouth. It was dirty, but Morry would recognize it anywhere. Wagging his tail excitedly, Fred knew he had gotten it right by the recognition in Morry's eyes. Morry took the bag from Fred, but soon thereafter had his breath taken away by the strong odor of dog pee. Apparently, Fred had marked the backpack as his own, as animals often do. Morry quickly unzipped the bag and secured its contents. Because the backpack was moisture-proof, the lotto ticket was intact and unsoiled. He immediately threw away the toothbrush in a nearby waste receptacle. The pencils and sketch pad, he kept.

"Little gangsta, you done good!" Morry had taken to referring to Fred as a gangster.

"Let's see what we've got to eat!" Morry took out the now-familiar box, which Fred looked forward to seeing every day. Wagging his tail excitedly, Fred jumped up on the bench. Morry opened the box and moved several feet away.

Fred was so hungry, he didn't notice that Morry had moved several feet away. After eating, Fred took off in the opposite direction, as usual wagging his tail.

That evening, upon returning to the overpass, Morry greeted Ben with the good news.

"Guess what? Fred came through! He brought the backpack to the park bench."

"Well, where is it?"

"Man, that thing was so filthy, I had to throw it away. As soon as I left the park, I went to the gas station to wash up. But I was happy to get my government phone and art supplies!"

"Well, good for you! I wonder what's going to happen to Fred now that he has a price on his head!"

"It's not that bad, Ben. You make it sound like they're going to execute him."

"Well, that's pretty much what's going to happen if they deem him a threat to himself and others, or if no one adopts him. But first they'll have to determine whether he's safe to adopt. After all, that dog has been living on the street."

Morry still hadn't told Ben about the lotto ticket. While at the gas station he checked the lotto ticket. It wasn't a jackpot winner, but it was worth a hundred thousand dollars. That would be enough for him to get an apartment and have time to try to market and sell his art. If his art wasn't profitable, he might have to return to the workforce.

The next day, Morry went looking for an apartment in the same general area. He found a small efficiency apartment for eight hundred dollars a month. This was perfect timing. The weather was changing and Ben had decided to move back in with his sister sooner than Thanksgiving.

That afternoon, Morry went to the bench. He waited for Fred, but the mutt never showed up. Morry asked around, enlisting Ben's assistance. As best he could tell, Fred had either been apprehended by the Humane Society or injured somewhere on the street.

Morry decided to go directly to the Humane Society. "No, we haven't seen him, but if we do, we're going to have to put him down. His owner came in and declared him to be a threat to himself and others!"

"That's unreal. What evidence did he give that Fred's a threat? Has he physically hurt anyone or endangered anyone, bit anyone? What has he done?!" Morry was appalled that a decision to take another life, even if nonhuman, could be made so lightly.

The Humane Society manager responded, "The owner filled out this form detailing the behavior of the dog while in his home and under his care. Also, other residents in the neighborhood have filed reports regarding thefts, vandalism, and more, naming Fred as the perp. Without supervision and direction, it's just a matter of time before this dog causes serious harm."

"What if he was off the street,…in a home?" Morry toyed with the idea of trying to get Fred into a home, not necessarily his home. Morry had never owned a pet, except for a goldfish when he was a child. Responsibility for something with four feet that required grooming, toileting, and other care did not appeal to him.

"I don't know where that would be. This dog's rep is all over the neighborhood. Being the terror that he is, he's become somewhat of a legend . . . a villain of sorts, public enemy number 1. But, yeah, if someone could take him in and keep him off of the street, he could be granted a stay."

With this in mind, Morry left his name and phone number with the manager, and continued to watch for Fred. He wasn't hanging out at Handler's and no one had seen him.

On a whim, Morry decided to retrace the blocks that Fred had taken him down several weeks before, when he was trying to retrieve Morry's property.

Morry looked in the backyard of the old, abandoned house where Fred had dug up the sweater, but there was no sign of him. The hole that he had dug was only partially covered, with the sleeve of the sweater peeking out. Morry continued on. He could only assume that this area was Fred's stomping ground and something serious must have happened to make Fred miss their daily luncheon. Morry continued to the next house where he recalled Fred stopping. Much to his disappointment, there was no Fred. Morry didn't know where else to look, so he went back to the bench. He sat there for a while, reminiscing about the smelly little dog whom he had initially found so contemptible. Now, much to his surprise, his days were occupied with thoughts about the whereabouts of the little fleabag.

Three days later, Morry returned to the Humane Society to see if anyone had located Fred.

"Oh, yeah, we picked him up yesterday. This is a smart dog. Once he figured out we were after him, he laid low. This dog has street smarts!"

"How come someone didn't notify me before now?"

"Mr. Allen, we had no way of getting in touch with you. The phone number you left was inactive."

Morry didn't know why his government phone was inactive, but he would deal with that later. He was too excited to be angry. "Well, where is he?"

"Follow me." The manager led him to the back room, where there were multiple dogs of various sizes and pedigrees.

"I don't see Fred."

"There he is." The manager led him to a cage in the back. As soon as the dog saw him, he started jumping up and down, wagging his tail. Fred didn't look like the Fred he knew. This dog was beautiful. He looked exactly like the dog on the poster with a reward of a thousand dollars.

"Yeah, he does look different, but we couldn't let him stay here without cleaning him up and grooming him. That dog had a scent that would stop a skunk at fifty paces! He was scheduled to be euthanized yesterday, but he cleaned up so well, I couldn't bring myself to do it. I just think we should still be able to find him a home!"

At that point, Morry decided that Fred was his dog. "I can provide a home. He can live with me."

"No offense, mister, but my understanding is that you're homeless. This dog needs to be domiciled and disciplined."

"I have secured a lease on an apartment and will be moving in in two days. If you just give me two days to move in and one day to set things up for Fred, I'll take him off your hands!"

The manager reluctantly agreed. "If you can bring a signed lease to the office tomorrow, the dog is yours. But be warned: if he ends up on the street again, he's a goner."

"Thank you! Thank you!" Morry was elated. "Did you hear that, Fred? You'll be going home."

Fred barked and wagged his tail, responding to Morry's excitement. However, he didn't understand why Morry left without him. He thought Morry was there to get him. Morry did return the next day, bringing snacks and the lease he had promised the manager.

Morry came to the Humane Society the next two days to see Fred, until he was ready to move into his apartment. This was a minimal feat since he had only a few belongings and several changes of clothing. Living on the street, he had managed to live on less than the basics.

The third day, he arrived as soon as the building opened at 9:00 a.m. sharp. The Humane Society donated a dog carrier to ensure that Fred wouldn't run away while Morry was taking him home.

The next week was blissful. Morry sketched pictures of Fred, of wildflowers in the park, and of other still life. He had bought a leash to try to acclimate Fred to being in tow. But in that second week, things started to change. Morry noticed that Fred seemed to be a little restless whenever he was on the leash. When walking Fred, Morry tried to direct him to go in a specific direction. If Fred's attention was elsewhere, he would pull away and tug in the direction of his focus.

Fred's rebellious spirit was starting to show up and show out. Morry didn't know if he was going to be able to tame the wild spirit in this dog.

One day, when Morry went to the door to get the newspaper, Fred bolted past him and ran outside.

"Well, I'll be—" Morry was speechless. At first, he started to put on his coat and go looking for Fred, but decided against

176

it. If the foolish dog didn't want to be kept, there was nothing he could do.

A week later, Morry opened the door to go for a walk. There was Fred, a little worse for wear, but still recognizable with his white fluffy coat, now a little gray. He trotted into the house and laid down on his doggy bed. Morry went to the cabinet and opened a can of Fred's favorite dog food. Fred ate the meal greedily and fell asleep on the floor.

Morry then proceeded to take his walk. Ben was no longer on the street since it was well into November, but he still kept in touch with Morry by phone.

Morry called Ben to catch up with him. They decided to meet at the Grease Spot for lunch.

"Hey, Morry. How's it going? Being off the street definitely agrees with you! I also heard that Fleabag Fred is living with you."

"Yes, but Ben, he's more than a handful; he's two handfuls. The sad part is that if I can't tame this dog and keep him off the street, he'll probably end up in the morgue."

"He just has to learn some discipline. Have you considered trying to enroll him in a dog etiquette and training class?"

"Now, you know that didn't work before. Remember, the prior owner stated that the dog ran away?"

"Yeah, but there were other things going on, too. The dog was forced to wear clothes and had pressure sores from being over-petted. No self-respecting dog would put up with that."

Morry could see that Ben was trying to inject a little humor into the situation, but his spirit wasn't lifted in the least.

That evening, Morry returned. Fred was still asleep. Fred must really be tired, Morry thought. He knew all too well that living on the street is a hard job. Morry put water in Fred's bowl in case he woke up thirsty in the middle of the night.

The next day, Morry awakened and fixed breakfast, including his favorite beverage of coffee mixed with hot chocolate, something he couldn't get easily when he was living on the street.

He opened the door to get his morning paper, as usual. This time he hesitated in the doorway. He looked at Fred and kept the door open. If Fred wanted to leave, Morry wasn't going to run after him or come looking for him.

Fred walked to the door slowly. He looked out, then looked up at Morry and headed back to his doggy bed. Just knowing he could leave when he got ready was enough for him to stay. Yes, this was home.

Morry contemplated trying to get Fred disciplined and trained. The more he thought about Ben's suggestion, the better it sounded. Morry went online to look for reputable trainers. Since Fred was a pedigreed dog, Morry wanted to find a trainer familiar with Pomeranians. Thank goodness Fred was housebroken. Morry also had to be mindful that the lotto money would not last indefinitely. He hadn't made any progress with getting his art displayed on consignment. At the very least, Fred needed to get vaccinated.

After making a vet appointment for the next day, Morry started to feel better. It was getting easier to get Fred into the carrier once Fred realized that every trip in the carrier didn't result in something unpleasant. Morry started to check with the previous owner to determine if Fred's vaccines were up to date, but decided against it. He wasn't sure how to approach him. It might be awkward. After all, Fred's prior owner had tried to have him euthanized.

Dr. Brown's nurse met Morry and Fred at the door. Fred seemed to warm up to the nurse right away, wagging his tail as soon as he heard her voice.

"Hi, little fellow! He's just so cute, Mr. Allen!" Melodie looked closer. "Has he been here before? He looks so familiar!" She peered into the dog's eyes and concluded, "It's Fred!"

Just then, Dr. Brown walked into the lobby. Morry had taken Fred out of the carrier.

"Hey, buddy! And hello, Mr. Allen! We haven't seen Fred in almost a year," he stated, addressing Morry. "What happened to Mr. Foxbourough?" Dr. Brown responded to Morry's puzzled look, "He was the previous owner".

"When he didn't bring Fred in to complete his vaccines, we called him. He stated that Fred had run away. He thought Fred might be a show Pomeranian. I agreed and offered to sponsor him as long as we could feature Fred on our posters for the clinic and our veterinary hospital. He told me that he had offered a reward for Fred, but after the first return, Fred ran away a second time. We certainly didn't think we would be seeing Fred again. I'm happy we were wrong."

"Well, to make a long story short, I rescued Fred from the street, and I'm the new owner."

"Good news. Fred only needs two more vaccines, so I'll offer you the same opportunity. In exchange for Fred being our poster dog or mascot, we'll pay for his training and provide free medical care. If you want to pursue dog competition, we'll cover those expenses, and would also ask for 50 percent of Fred's winnings, if there should be any."

"Well, let's get Fred vaccinated, and I'll think about it." Morry was in no hurry to commit Fred to any arrangement that he may not be able to tolerate. Fred had been through a lot, and Morry felt an obligation to make it up to him by not repeating Foxbourough's mistakes.

Examining Fred with care and thoroughness, Dr. Brown gained Morry's confidence. Before they left the office, the vet made another pitch. "You know, Fred has something, a certain je ne sais quoi. It translates through the camera. He could sell anything, not just our clinic. Let me show you something!" Dr. Brown pulled out Fred's folder, which contained a picture taken at Fred's first visit. His big eyes were bright, sparkling, and full of life. Morry could swear that Fred was smiling. That must have been before Fred started running away, Morry thought.

By now, Melodie had placed Fred back in the carrier, and he was anxious to get home.

"We'll think about it, doc." Morry was very excited about the prospect of getting Fred's medical care covered by Dr. Brown. After all, he couldn't afford ongoing vet care; he didn't even have medical coverage for himself.

He was going to run it past Ben to see what he thought. He might even discuss it with his parents. He hadn't spoken to them in months, but he was so excited about getting his apartment that he'd called his dad the Friday before. They'd decided to meet up for breakfast for old times' sake. So, Morry was looking forward to breakfast as he awakened at 7:00 a.m. He wanted to get up earlier to see the sunrise. This was a pleasure that he looked forward to, but he overslept. When he was living on the street, he never saw the sunrise while sleeping under the overpass. Now, he liked to sit in the kitchen and drink his chocolate-coffee while he watched the sun appear.

Living indoors had its perks!

At 8:00 a.m., Ben arrived, to dog-sit, with Fred's favorite dog food and a few dog treats. Normally, Morry would have left Fred at home alone, but he wanted Ben to spend time with Fred to help him sense Fred's mindset. Ben had become a sort of dog whisperer for Morry. He had been visiting Morry for some time now, and he was good at figuring out how Fred was feeling or why he was more difficult at some times than others. Matter of fact, Ben was the one who first determined that Fred had run away after becoming too overwhelmed by the baggage the Foxbouroughs had loaded onto him. This was long before he had ever met Fred. Now Morry wanted to get Ben's opinion about whether he should consider grooming Fred for pet competitions.

"Hey, Morry! Man, you look good! Domestication agrees with you. I didn't think you could be housebroken!"

Morry laughed as he welcomed Ben in. Fred, hearing Ben, rushed into the room. He knew that, as usual, Ben had a treat or two for him. Fred jumped up and down, wagging his

181

tail as he followed the visitor and his burlap bag to the kitchen. Fred had come to recognize the bag as the bearer of good news.

"Wow, Fred has really taken to you, and the fact that you bring him treats hasn't hurt at all. Yet I still wonder how you do it!"

"It's not a mystery. Animals are like people. They have feelings, too. Sometimes, if you want to know what they might be thinking, just put yourself in their place. For instance, when Foxbourough first described Fred's role in their household, it just sounded like a lot of responsibility. I can't imagine being responsible for the needs of three people, let alone one . . . and they were expecting this one poor mutt to make them all happy! Try doing that day in and day out!" Ben bent down to hand Fred a treat as he excitedly jumped up and down between the two men.

"Well, I took Fred to the vet a few days ago, and he thinks Fred would be a natural as a show dog, but I don't want to give Fred any reason to hit the streets again. So I wanted to get your opinion."

"I don't know a lot about it, but I understand that the training and the grooming can be very expensive."

"Dr. Brown offered to sponsor Fred and provide his medical care, for half of any prize money Fred might win."

"How did he determine all of that about Fred at one visit?"

"The irony of it is that he had been taking care of Fred before he ran away, when Foxbourough was Fred's owner.

What are the odds that I would end up taking Fred to the same doctor he was seeing before he ran away?"

"Yeah, how did you choose Dr. Brown?"

"Mostly it was convenience. Since I don't have a car and Fred and I travel mostly on foot or by public transportation, I was looking for someone close, but I had also checked around with some of the neighbors, who gave Dr. Brown the thumbs up. So I guess Fred and I lucked out." After pausing to look at his watch, Morry turned toward the door. "I'm going to have to leave, Ben. It's going to take me about thirty minutes to walk to the Grease Spot, but you and Fred have fun, and you can tell me what you think of Dr. Brown's offer later."

Ben closed the door behind Morry and turned on the TV as he tossed Fred his Raggedy Ann doll. Ben marveled at how well the doll had cleaned up—almost as well as Fred. When the Humane Society had captured Fred, he'd had the doll in his mouth, and they weren't able to get it away from him. So when they washed Fred, they washed the doll as well since it was aggressively gripped in his mouth. From what Ben could recall, this was the doll Fred had dug up and presented to Morry that day he led him around the neighborhood before determining which of his buried treasures belonged to Morry. While watching TV, Ben came across an old Lassie movie on the TV. Fred paused and started to bark at the screen. It wasn't aggressive or angry. It was as if Fred was trying to talk to or communicate with the dog on the other side of the screen.

"Really, Fred?" Ben laughed at the thought that Fred might actually have something important to say to Lassie, like "Girl, don't you let them work you to death. Timmie will come home on his own!" Lassie was a popular dog TV personality back in the day. Lassie was unofficially charged with the family's safety; especially the youngest son, Timmie. The notion that Fred could be a celebrity too was not an impossibility to Ben. Ben continued to toss toys for Fred to retrieve. Then he decided to see if he could teach Fred a few simple tricks.

"Follow me, Fred." Ben walked around the room several times. Fred followed Ben with his eyes, but nothing else. Then Ben took a treat and repeated the same command. Fred's eyes fixated on the treat, and the rest of him followed. After Fred followed him around the room three times, Ben gave up the treat. He would have tried for a fourth time, but Fred was starting to get impatient and nip at his heels. His little legs didn't allow him to jump high enough to grab the snack that was well outside of his reach. Ben did this several times, until finally he decided to substitute approval or praise for the treat. After a time, Fred was following him by command even without a treat in his hand. Ben made sure that when he didn't give Fred a treat, he patted him or hugged him and said, "Good dog!"

"You're special, Fred! I knew it the day you lapped up that beer. Any dog that drinks beer and lives to bark about it is a dog after my own heart!" Fred was wagging his tail frantically, expecting another treat based on Ben's approving tone. After all, he didn't know what Ben was saying. Or did he? Ben wondered.

* * * * * * *

Meanwhile, Morry approached the "Grease Spot", with some trepidation. He wanted his parents to know that he was happier, in the past weeks, than he had been in the past few years. However, he wanted to avoid any controversy about his chosen life paths. Coming into the diner entry, he saw his parents sitting quietly, staring into the distance. Usually their eyes would light up with recognition, upon his arrival. They always arrived first, anticipating a favorable outcome, in their attempts to entice him back home. This time was different.

"Hi, Morry", his dad was the first to speak, saddened by the prospect of the ensuing conversation.

"Morry, sweetheart, how are you doing?", his mother chimed in.

"I'm fine....but why the long faces?' Morry began to imagine the unimaginable. Before he could torture himself any longer, his dad cleared his throat.

"Son, I've been diagnosed with Alzheimers. I'm in the early stages, but for months now, I've noticed that I've been forgetting simple tasks and familiar places and people. The doctors can't predict how rapidly it will progress. I would like to enjoy the time that I have left being in a good place with you. So if you're happy, and I speak for your mom, as well, we'er happy.

Morry's mind was in chaos. Reflecting back on subtle clues that he may have picked up on, during the past few breakfasts, he felt selfish. He never considered what was going on in his parent's lives, while defending his life style. They ordered and ate in silence. After approximately 10 minutes, Morry lightened the air.

"I'm getting involved in dog show competitions." Morry proceeded to tell his parents about Fred and rescuing him from the shelter. Both his parents seemed relieved to change the topic of conversation. They were amused at the episode of Fred stealing cupcakes and drinking beer on the street.

At the conclusion of breakfast, Morry walked his parents to their car. He hugged them both, not wanting to let go. He wanted them to always be there and to never change. But he knew that this was an impossibility. He resolved to check with his parents in between breakfasts to see if they needed anything. He also let them know, at this point, that he would consider moving back home, if they needed him. The senior Allens assured him that this was not necessary. All they had ever wanted was for him to come home, so he thought, and now that he was willing too do so, they declined. This was strange! What Morry didn't realize was that they wanted him safe. And now that he was domiciled the details were unimportant, as long as, he was safe.

When Morry returned, Fred and Ben were perched in front of the TV. "I hope you two haven't been sitting in front of the TV the whole time I've been gone. Ben, you're going to spoil that dog."

"Too late. The next time I come, I'm going to bring a six pack, for Fred and I, to watch the game." Morry knew that Ben was joking since they both knew that Fred's previous encounter with the beer truck could have been fatal.

"What game?"

"Whatever game is on. You don't need a special occasion to drink a good beer! But let me show you something." He stood. "Follow me, Fred!" Ben started walking and Fred quickly fell into step and followed him around the room until he stopped. He then petted Fred and praised him. This was an accomplishment for Fred, who for the most part was being

186

transported by carrier. Morry didn't trust Fred to follow him, but Ben had proven that Fred was trainable.

Morry smiled, knowing that dumpster diving and a professional dog show were worlds apart, and it would take a lot to advance Fred from the former to the latter. However, Morry had seen enough to be hopeful. He had gone online to get additional information regarding dog shows and found out that the Platinum Kennel Dog exhibition was among the elite of dog competitions. If he was going to do this with Fred, he wanted him to be ready to compete at the highest level.

After a week of contemplation, Morry called Dr. Brown. "Hey, doc, I've thought about your proposition, and I think it might be doable. But, first, let's just start with taking pictures of Fred for the clinic and go from there. He's been living on the street and has a wild streak. So we need to see if he can cooperate with something as simple as a photo shoot."

"Okay, Morry. Let's set an appointment for two weeks from now. I'll have our clinic photographer come in, and we'll go from there."

Immediately after speaking with Dr. Brown, Morry called Ben. "I did it! I set up an appointment with Dr. Brown for a photo shoot for Fred. So I need you to help me get him ready."

"What do you mean, get him ready? All he has to do is sit still and let the photographer position him and pose him."

"Exactly. Fred may not react well to being handled after a year on the street."

"Well, he does okay with you."

187

"Yeah, but I'm not posing him or putting a camera in his face or having him sit under bright lights."

"Relax, Morry. It'll be fine. After all, Fred sat still long enough to develop pressure sores after a young child was too aggressive with petting him. He'll do fine! Also, try to get him used to being around other dogs. He seems to be rather social. Try letting him look at dogs on TV. This will be the least threatening, initially, and then start taking him to a dog park to interact with other dogs."

"Wow, Ben, that's good advice. What did you say you used to do before you retired? Did you ever work with animals?"

"No, Morry. I worked at a desk job, crunching numbers. I feel as if the best years of my life were spent indoors, counting someone else's money. I was an accountant. One day, I'd had enough, and I closed the doors of my practice and decided I was going to spend as much time outdoors as possible. I got to the point where I didn't want any responsibility for anything or anyone. So I never got married or formed any attachments that might make me accountable to anyone else."

"That sounds lonely."

"Believe you me, I'm anything but lonesome. I'm good company. Whenever I feel like I might be missing out on something, I go to visit my sister and I stay with her during the winter months. I watch her struggle to pay bills and raise two kids on her nursing salary, and then I count my blessings!"

Morry thought this was pretty dismal. Measuring his own happiness based on how miserable someone else was didn't seem to be a true measure of happiness, but he kept this to himself. He valued Ben's friendship and hadn't stayed close with any of his previous friends since living on the street.

Morry also wondered why Ben hadn't asked him where he got the funds to get his apartment. He was starting to feel guilty about not mentioning the lotto ticket since Ben had helped him track down Fred. He decided that in some kind of way, he would make it up to Ben. In the meantime, he wouldn't bring up any details about funding his apartment unless Ben asked.

The next two weeks went by in a whirlwind. Fred continued to sketch and went to several Hyde Park galleries to see if he could display his art on consignment. But even that required depositing money to rent the space. Again, he had to budget his lotto winnings very carefully. Fred was doing well and starting to gain weight. Morry needed to be careful not to let Fred gain too much, and then have to worry about him not being considered show-worthy.

The day of Fred's photo shoot, they arrived at the clinic thirty minutes early. Morry was so excited, he'd barely slept the night before and was actually up before sunrise, sitting at his kitchen table with his chocolate coffee.

Melodie greeted them at the door. "Come on in! Can I get you something? Water, coffee?"

"No, we're fine. Thanks."

"Okay, well, follow me back to the conference room. The photographer is setting up there."

Walking down the hallway, Morry wondered if he had prepared Fred for an experience that might not be completely to Fred's liking. To this end, Morry had decided that if Fred showed any signs of distress or discomfort, he would terminate the session and look for other ways to pay for Fred's health care and upkeep.

As the door opened, Morry saw a water bowl in the corner with a bag of treats, and a backdrop with a photo spotlight. Fred ran straight to the bag of doggy treats.

"Hold on, Fred. Those might not be for you."

"Of course they're for Frederico," the photographer laughed.

She was not what Morry had expected. He'd assumed the photographer was going to be a man. Why he'd made that assumption, he didn't know, since he was well aware of many world-famous woman photographers.

"My name is Maia Mitchell. I took Fred's picture a year ago for his medical file. It occurred to me back then that he was extraordinarily photogenic, and that was just with standard lighting and the usual settings. But now we're going to do something special with Frederico to highlight his best features. Dr. Brown believes that he can be the face of Brown Clinic, and I do too."

The fact that Maia had worked with Fred before made Morry feel better. Fred definitely appeared to remember her since he started to wag his tail and jump up and down as soon as he saw her. Morry had a good feeling about the way Fred's future was unfolding.

After choosing the best lighting and backdrop for Fred's pictures, Maia took several shots with Dr. Brown pretending to examine Fred. In each photo, looking closely would reveal that Dr. Brown had a treat poised in the opposite hand, ready to reward Fred after each successfully executed photo. After about forty-five minutes, the session was over, and everyone seemed happy. Fred was watered and well fed, and Maia had the shots that she thought best highlighted the services of the clinic, with Fred as the happy patient.

"You're really good at this. I was apprehensive about the experience Fred might have, but it was all good!" Morry was totally impressed.

Maia mused, "Really, Mr. Allen? This is my job. I had better be good at it if I expect to pay my bills. Of course, as you cover a variety of subjects, you become more adaptable to various subjects and settings."

"What do you mean?" Morry wanted to know more.

"Well, I didn't always photograph animals. Before meeting Dr. Brown, I had only human subjects, but once he hired me to take photos for his clinic, I adapted to working with animals and their owners. Some of the owners have hired me to take family photos that were mostly centered around their pets, as opposed to their families. Sometimes they will request photos for Christmas cards or other holiday cards. Now that you've picked my brain, tell me, how do you pay your bills?" Maia didn't know why she had spent the better part of thirty minutes, beyond the time that she was being paid for, to talk with Morry, but he seemed truly interested in her work.

"I'm a wannabe artist, so I have yet to pay any bills from it. But it's my passion." Morry avoided mentioning that he had been homeless. This was not a topic that would contribute to making a good first impression.

191

"Are you any good?"

"I guess I won't really know until I sell something! Or I could get your opinion." Morry hesitated. "If you have some time, I could take you to lunch one day and bring my portfolio." Morry actually did want someone else's opinion, but it didn't hurt that Maia was pretty and intelligent. He didn't bother to find out if she was available, but since he didn't see a ring, he felt safe assuming that she wasn't married and, at the very least, wasn't engaged.

"Okay. I'll be back in this area next week. How about lunch at Corey's Café on Monday, twelve thirty sharp? And be sure to bring your portfolio."

Morry looked puzzled. Maia responded, "Oh, you'd be surprised how many guys want to 'show me something,' and then conveniently forget their work. Then they think I'm going to follow them back to their apartment to see what they should have brought with them."

Morry laughed, "Oh, no! I'm not that guy! I really do want your opinion!"

"Good! I'll see you then!"

All this time, Fred laid in the corner, taking a nap. Morry was so engrossed in his conversation with Maia, he hadn't noticed that Fred had dozed off. All of those treats probably made him sluggish, Morry thought. He gently placed Fred in his carrier and took him home. If he'd had a leash, he would have awakened Fred for the walk so he could get some much-needed exercise.

When they arrived home, it was past 4:00 p.m. Morry thought the day had gone well and called Ben to give him the 411.

"Hey, Morry. How'd it go?"

"Man, it went so well, I couldn't have planned it better. The photographer was awesome and Fred cooperated completely. I think this might work out. I'm totally excited!"

Ben was curious to know why Morry was so excited about one photo session. But he kept this to himself. If there was more to tell, Morry would tell him in due time. Ben was not one to pry. He did, however, wonder where Morry had gotten the money to move into an apartment after living on the street for months. But this, too, he figured Morry would disclose when he was ready.

Over the remainder of the week, Morry worked frantically to add additional sketches to his collection in order to justify taking up someone else's time, someone whose opinion he valued.

He had sketched Fred in various states of slumber. This was the only time Fred stayed still long enough to be sketched. He had drawings of still life and sunsets. There were no humans since he hadn't spent much time interacting with others, except for Ben. Because of this, he felt as if he was somewhat of a cheat or fraud. In his opinion, artists couldn't truly say they had mastered the art of sketching until they were able to capture the essence of emotion or feeling on paper to be felt by others. Of course, there were masters who specialized in landscapes and other subjects, so this was just his opinion.

193

At lunch that next week, Maia arrived early. Power play or not, she wanted to be able to leave early if things went south, without feeling guilty. This was best accomplished by making the other party feel as if they had kept her waiting, even if they were on time.

At twelve thirty sharp, Morry came through the door, all smiles. In natural light, she could tell that he was older than she'd originally thought, but that wasn't a bad thing: he actually looked not just older, but distinguished.

"Hey, good to see you again!" Morry greeted Maia as he sat down at the table. "This was a good choice. I haven't been here in years." After looking over the menu, Morry was happy to see that the prices hadn't changed much either.

Maia was relieved to see that Morry had his black oversized binder under his left arm. So he really was looking to get her opinion.

After they ordered Reuben sandwiches, fries, and sides, they settled into more relaxed conversation. Interestingly enough, they'd both decided on the same side in addition to incidentally choosing the same sandwich. Morry didn't know if this meant something, but if nothing else, Maia would be a good friend to have.

"So, let's see what you got!" Maia reached for the binder. Laying it out on the table, she pored over each scene, periodically pausing to comment. "Oh, this is nice . . . interesting . . . hmm."

Morry was disappointed that she didn't seem particularly impressed with any of his work, even the pictures of Fred. "You don't seem to be excited or impressed with any of my work. Tell me what you're thinking."

194

"Well, impressed isn't the word. Your technical skills are good. The dimensions and details are good, but there's no energy or life force being transmitted. Meaning, I'm not moved. Your work is pleasant, but not compelling. That's hard to capture when doing still-life scenes, so I get it, but even Fred's picture is boring. Maybe because you sketched him while he was asleep, but even then, the stillness or calm that comes with sleep isn't being transmitted."

Morry was visibly hurt, but tried to disguise his feelings. After all, Maia was just a photographer. What did she know? But he couldn't be mad at her; he asked for her opinion and she gave it freely. Almost too freely for his liking. However, maybe living on the street had deprived him of his ability to connect to and channel his talent.

Swallowing hard to try to get the last bite of his Reuben to go down, he took a gulp of his raspberry tea.

"Look, Morry, I'm just one person, but if you're interested in talking to my brother, he can probably give you a better perspective. He's an accomplished artist. Maison started painting when he was twelve—"

"Wait! Maison Mitchell is your brother?!" Morry couldn't believe his ears.

"Why, yes. I take it you're familiar with his work. He started painting when he was twelve years old, and sold his first painting at fifteen. As a result, he continued to progress in his craft and paid his way through art school. He also paid my college tuition, bought my parents a home, and the list goes on. You know, I think the two of you may be about the same age." This was Maia's way of trying to find out Morry's age without asking directly.

A little embarrassed, Morry admitted, "I'm forty-three." He waited to get her reaction since he knew that at some point he was going to have to explain why he was such a late bloomer.

Maia smiled. "Yes, I guessed about right. Maison's forty-four . . . and, in case you were wondering, I'm thirty-three."

Morry was relieved that Maia, although younger than he, was not as young as he had initially thought. Because of her youthful appearance, he'd suspected she was maybe twenty-six or twenty-seven. So it wasn't implausible that she might be somewhat interested in him. He was very interested in her.

"So, here's what we'll do. Let me text some of your pictures to Maison and see what he thinks, and then he can call you directly. Let's pick out the ones you think are the best."

Maia carefully took photos of Morry's selections. She then texted them to her big brother with an attached message. "Hey M, got a new friend who is trying to get started. Here's a representation of his best work. Please let him know what you think." She put Morry's number at the end of the text.

"Now, Morry, he's really busy getting ready for a showing at a new gallery, but I know he'll get back to you. Because I don't make a habit of asking him to look at another artist's work, he'll know it's important."

"Thank you, Maia. You just don't know how much this means to me! You're very kind."

"Well, when Maison calls or texts you, and he will—I just don't know how soon—make sure you take advantage of any time or advice he gives you. It could be a make-or-break career move. He carries a lot of weight in the art world!"

Morry knew this to be true and reassured Maia that he wouldn't squander any opportunity he was given. He also decided that maybe his work wasn't as hopeless as he'd inferred from her initial response. She was at least willing to ask her brother to look at it.

As they parted, Maia asked Morry to call her back and let her know what Maison thought.

"I don't have your number."

"Yes, you do. I texted it to you after I sent your pictures to Maison. See you later!"

Morry watched as Maia walked away. It had been an unbelievable afternoon. What had started out as a casual lunch could possibly turn his life around. Art was his lifelong ambition.

The next day, Morry had new incentive. He decided he was going to try sketching Fred while he was awake, and even considered doing sketches from photos of Fred.

Since his day at the clinic for the photo shoot, Fred appeared to be more settled. The animal shows also seemed to soothe him. There weren't a lot of them on TV, so Morry had started streaming dog and other animal videos online. This meant upgrading his service. He had already chucked the government phone for a regular iPhone.

He had also taken Fred to the dog park several times. Fred was curious about the other dogs, but still hesitant to interact with them. Morry wondered about the outcome of Fred's photo shoot. He didn't have to wonder long.

Within a week's time, Dr. Brown forwarded the pictures of Fred to Morry. Included in the package was a contract detailing the agreement they had been discussing informally during the last two encounters. Morry looked over it, but wasn't comfortable with a lot of the legalities of what he thought should have been a simple agreement. This was important, so he decided to consult a lawyer. He spoke with Ben, who recommended his sister's lawyer.

The fee was reasonable, but still more than Morry was comfortable with since he didn't have a regular income.

The lawyer had recommended a clause that would allow Morry to terminate the contract if at any time he felt that the schedule or the work was too demanding. But in the event that occurred, Morry would have to pay a penalty for cancellation. Likewise, Dr. Brown could cancel the contract if he thought Fred wasn't living up to Morry's end of the bargain. The contract would last for five years, with possible renewal if agreed upon by both parties.

After Morry signed the contract, Fred's picture appeared in an ad for the Brown Veterinary Hospital and Clinic, and a life-sized picture of Fred was in the Brown Clinic window. This happened rather quickly.

Dr. Brown called Morry three weeks later. "Morry, that ad with Fred's picture has increased traffic through the clinic by 20 percent, and that's just been in the past three weeks. I can't imagine what's going to happen in the coming months."

After another three weeks, Dr. Brown suggested to Morry that Fred start working with a trainer in anticipation of competing in local dog shows. "Here are the names of three trainers who come highly recommended. Don't worry about the cost. As per the contract, the clinic will cover it."

"Okay, doc. I'll look into it, but I don't want to rush Fred."

"Yes, but he'll have to get started sometime, in order for us to determine if he is competition material."

Rather than make the decision himself, Morry took Fred with him in order to determine whether the dog had chemistry with any one particular trainer.

The first appointment was with a trainer who had been in the business for twenty-five years. He was a tall, gruff kind of man with a gravelly voice. When he greeted Fred and Morry at the door, Fred ran under the nearest chair and stayed there despite Morry tugging gently at his leash. Morry could only assume that the man's voice was what was upsetting to Fred. Morry knew that this was not a fit, and he slowly but gently lured Fred from under the chair with a treat. The second appointment several days later was better, but it still wasn't a match. The chemistry just wasn't there. Morry decided to wait another week before interviewing the third trainer. Fred had met two strangers in the last week, and he didn't want to upset Fred any more than necessary prior to finding the right trainer.

The third visit was much different. Upon arrival, Fred and Morry were taken into a small conference room that contained a box of animal toys in the corner and pictures of other famous dogs. Morry didn't assume that this trainer had worked with these dogs, but it seemed the trainer wanted the observer to infer as much.

After waiting fifteen minutes, Fred was starting to get restless despite having his Raggedy Ann doll to play with. As if on cue, a grandfatherly gentleman walked in. His voice was low, but soothing. He introduced himself as Jack Jonisen.

"Hello, Mr. Allen. I understand you're interested in getting your dog prepared to enter dog shows. Do you have any experience with the process?"

"No," Morry replied reluctantly.

"Well, that may be good or bad, depending on how you look at it. Not every pedigreed dog is show material." Jack began to pet Fred, absentmindedly it seemed, but was intentional about observing his general demeanor. Any dog that was standoffish, easily frightened, or easily provoked wasn't good material since some traits are hard to train away. Much to Fred's credit, he continued to play with Raggedy Ann and wag his tail.

To Jack, this was a good sign. "Tell you what: let's start Fred with the very basics and see how he does. We also have to take some formal measurements, weigh him, and so on, to see if he fits the profile of a show Pomeranian. He certainly is a pretty dog; his coat is healthy and full." If Jack had seen Fred a year ago, when he had pressure sores, he wouldn't have known this was the same dog.

So that was settled. He gave Mr. Jonisen the contact information for Dr. Brown for billing purposes. Things were moving along nicely for Fred. Morry just hoped it wasn't too fast. He was still waiting to hear back from Maison Mitchell. It had been some weeks, and he wanted to call Maia, but hesitated to do so until he had something to discuss. He didn't want to appear too anxious about seeing her again.

Weeks later, Maison Mitchell texted Morry. "Saw your work. I think you have promise. You may be using the wrong medium. Because your lines are soft, the colored pencils aren't allowing a distinct picture of your subject matter. Consider acrylics or oils for better clarity. Come to the M2 Gallery, 52nd and Blackstone, Friday at 3:30 p.m. I'm in town for one day."

Morry responded that he would be there. He didn't know if anything was on his agenda for that day, but if it was, he didn't need a calendar to know it would have to wait. Friday was only two days away.

Friday morning, Morry was already planning what he was going to wear, what he was going to say, trying to imagine how this encounter would play out. He had called his parents and Ben to advise them of this meeting the same day he received the text from Maison. Ben didn't know who Maison Mitchell was, but Morry's parents were aware of Mitchell's reputation as an artist and had followed his career to a certain degree. After a time, though, they'd stopped since it was a painful reminder that someone close to their son's age was such a success, while Morry still hadn't landed on his feet.

Morry had frequented the M2 Gallery in the past, but with no idea that he would ever get to meet Maison Mitchell. Arriving early, as he had always been advised to do for interviews and business meetings, Morry found the receptionist at the back of the gallery. He informed her that he had a meeting with Mr. Mitchell as he shifted his portfolio under his left arm to sign in.

"Right. He's expecting you, but he's on a call. Why don't you walk around the gallery, and I'll come and get you when he's ready?"

Morry was nervous, but decided that there was no reason to be. He was going to get advice from one artist to another. No pressure.

As he meandered around the gallery, he noticed that although Maison Mitchell used mostly oils, acrylics, and charcoals, there was a room dedicated to photos, mostly black and whites. He had been in this room before and found the work extraordinary, but never noticed that the first name of the photographer was Maia. He had never thought much about who this other Mitchell was, and now he realized that Maia was someone in her own right, as a photographer.

"Come this way, Mr. Allen."

Following obediently, they walked down a long corridor made of charcoal-gray glass, housing large offices on either side with interior glass walls as well. Everything was very ornate and expensive, as best Morry could tell.

As they arrived at the office at the end of the hallway, Morry could see a very tall figure walking toward the door, approximately six foot three, clothed in a suit worth about two thousand dollars and a tie that probably cost more than Morry's whole outfit, including his shoes. They entered the office and Morry came face-to-face with the larger-than-life Maison Mitchell. He could see the family resemblance. He had the same high cheekbones as Maia and a prominent forehead that Maia didn't have. Nonetheless, it was clear they were related.

"Good afternoon, Mr. Mitchell. Thank you for your time."

"Call me M. Let's get right to it. Maia thinks you may have talent, but I'm not sure. I think you have promise; there's a difference. Talent is an innate ability to create what was gifted to you in your genetic makeup. Promise is the possibility of talent, but it still isn't clear if by imitation or design you just happened at one time to create something that appeals to the majority of a group. Promise, if it's revealed to be talent, will repeat itself over and over again. Promise, if not true talent, is unpredictable and may have one or two successes, but nothing consistent. Speaking of which, how long have you been trying to get started?" Maison had looked at Morry and decided that, like himself, Morry was getting along in years and didn't have time to waste in pursuing anything he wasn't serious about.

"As far back as high school, I was interested in pursuing an art career, but I ended up going to medical school in deference to my parents. After two long years, I decided it wasn't for me and I dropped out. I had a short-lived real estate career that was profitable until the 2008 bust. I eventually lost everything and ended up homeless. Recently, I was able to secure an apartment. All this time, I've been using colored pencils to sketch since it's difficult to maintain art supplies when living on the street." Morry admitted all of this with embarrassment, but knew that if M was going to help him, he needed to be honest.

"And how did you meet Maia? Was she volunteering at a soup kitchen or something?"

Morry wasn't sure if this was shade or if M just had a wry sense of humor. "No, we met when she did a photo shoot for my dog at Dr. Brown's clinic."

"Oh, yeah. You're the owner of that Pomeranian she's crazy about. That dog has something; if he were a person, he'd be a star!"

This was the second or third time Morry had heard this about Fred, and he knew it was just a matter of time before Fred became the next Lassie if he played his cards right.

"I see you brought some more pictures. Can I look at them?" M reached for the portfolio that was now lying on his desk.

After perusing Morry's work for a moment, he said, "Okay, I see where you're going with this, but I don't know that anyone's going to like it once you get there! Morry—can I call you Morry?" Not waiting for a reply, Maison continued. "Your passion and desire to create art has to translate to the paper, canvas, or whatever backdrop you're using. Don't just sketch or paint something because it's there. You've got to create because you're driven to paint something or create art because the subject speaks to your soul. It has to move you. If it doesn't move you, what makes you think it's going to move anyone else? Look at each one of these pictures. Why did you create them? Did you sketch them because they spoke to you, or just because they were there?"

"Well—" Morry began hesitantly. He was somewhat taken aback by the frank manner in which Maison spoke to him, but he appreciated it. "When I was sketching on the streets, I didn't have time to think about what moved me. I thought more about where my next meal was coming from. Once I moved indoors, I was happy to be able to sit still long enough to sketch still life and not have to secure a place to sleep, and to be able to see the sunrise—"

"And did the sunrise move you, or the still life speak to your soul?" M interrupted.

"Not exactly," Morry admitted.

"So Morry, man, what speaks to you? What stirs your soul? What brings out the passion in your character that inspires you to create or replicate that item on paper, canvas, whatever?"

"I guess I don't know. I hadn't thought about it like that."

"You need to search your soul before you waste any more time on pictures that are going to be inconsequential. If you just want to sketch or paint as a hobby, these are fine. But if you're going to create and be a great artist and you have talent, you've got to commit to the passion of the art and create what inspires you, what speaks to you. Once you've found that, you'll be driven, and you'll live to create. Every project will be a new adventure. Maia mentioned that she didn't feel any life force or energy in your sketches, but the correct word for it is *passion*! Find it, and you'll be on your way to greatness!"

Morry was dazed. He felt as if he had been run over by an eighteen-wheeled tractor trailer. He mumbled his thanks to Maison and gathered up his pictures.

"Don't be discouraged, Morry. Just find your passion. Call me back in a month or so and we can speak again. But if you don't find the passion, be honest with yourself and move on."

Morry walked back to his apartment, reflecting on what M had said. He wanted to be able to think back to when he'd first decided he wanted to be an artist. Although he'd been only sixteen years old at the time, something must have spoken to his soul. He needed to recapture what that was. Over the years of doing what others had wanted him to do and trying to make a living, he had lost that spark, that passion, that M spoke about.

As Morry walked up the stairs and opened the door, Fred came running toward him, jumping up and down and wagging his tail. At first Morry just thought Fred was happy to see him. Then he realized poor Fred was probably hungry. In his haste to get to the gallery early, Morry had forgotten to set out Fred's dinner and put water in his bowl. After opening a can of Fred's favorite food and filling his bowl with fresh water, Morry sat down.

He was tired. He wanted to talk with someone and have a light, inconsequential conversation, but he knew that wasn't possible. Everyone he considered calling would want to know how his meeting with Maison Mitchell had gone, and he wasn't ready to discuss it just yet. Morry was tired! He hadn't been this tired since he was out on the streets looking for Fred after the Humane Society had put a price on the rebellious dog's head.

Morry went to bed early after taking a nice, warm shower. Ah, the luxury of living indoors.

Over the next two weeks, Morry thought about his passion. He realized it wasn't just one thing. He cared about animals, he cared about justice, about fairness, and it didn't necessarily involve painting animals or pictures of what justice looked like. He knew justice and injustice when he saw them, and he didn't need to paint them to feel passionate about them.

He remembered how incensed and enraged he'd felt when the Humane Society had suggested that Fred might be put down just because he was out on the street due to an insensitive owner who didn't know how to take care of him. The next day he called the Animal Welfare League. Morry decided he was going to become an advocate for animal rights. He still wasn't sure how he was going to support himself, but right now he felt good about his decision.

He still continued to sketch, but there was no pressure. He was doing it strictly for fun. He also made another decision he had been putting off for some time. He needed to let Ben know about the lotto ticket he had cashed in months before. He wasn't sure how much he should give Ben, but he knew he owed him something. Ben had helped him pursue the leads that resulted in his finding Fred. Having made this decision, Morry decided that he didn't want to put it off one more minute. He called Ben, to catch up.

While Morry was on the phone, Fred was rolling around on the floor, playing with Raggedy Ann. "Hey, man, you never told me what happened at your meeting with Maison Mitchell. Is he going to mentor you, or display your works at one of his galleries?"

Morry laughed. "Nah. He told me essentially that I had no passion, and if I couldn't find it, I might as well not waste my time."

"Wow. How did that make you feel? You've only wanted to be an artist since you were sixteen years old."

"It made me think. I reexamined my priorities and determined that there was something more important to me than being an artist: animal rights."

207

"So, how are you going to support yourself? Matter of fact, I've often wondered how you were able to move off the street and take in Fred once you retrieved your backpack."

"That's why I wanted to talk to you. Months ago, when we were looking for Fred, I didn't tell you that the backpack contained a lotto ticket someone had dropped into my panhandler's cup. It wasn't a grand prize winner, but it was a hundred thousand dollars; enough for me to get an efficiency apartment. Morry cringed at the thought that Ben might ask for half, since he no longer had enough left to give Ben half of the original money. He did have some income from the dog shows that Fred had been winning.

Ben was quiet for a moment. "You know, I often wondered why you were so obsessed with getting that backpack returned, but I didn't press you on it because I figured you'd tell me in good time. I guess now is a good time." Ben sounded morose.

Morry was sad. He hadn't felt this bad since his hopes of becoming an artist were dashed by Maison Mitchell. Fred, sensing a change in Morry's mood, went back to his doggy bed, and laid down.

"Well, Ben, how about I give you ten thousand? That would be 10 percent."

"Morry, do you even have ten thousand dollars?"

"Well, barely, but I need to make this right. I've been thinking about it ever since I cashed the ticket in."

"So to make it right, you'd give me your last funds and risk you and Fred living on the street again? I won't have it!"

The tension in Morry's body relaxed. "I don't need the money, Morry. I live on the street by choice. I have savings. So keep the money, and if we're going to continue to be friends, just always be honest with me."

He let out an inaudible sigh. "Okay, man, you got it!"

The next thirty days flew by as Morry took Fred to the trainer several times a week. According to Jack, Fred was doing really well, and he wanted Morry to enter Fred in one of the local junior competitions. He thought Fred would be ready.

Morry told Ben, who was equally excited. In his preparation for Fred's first show, Morry forgot to call Maia back to tell her about the meeting with M. So when he saw a text from her, he quickly remembered his promise. He responded quickly, but succinctly, that M felt he needed to find his passion.

Maia responded, "Don't worry! You will!" He wanted to ask her out on a real date, but was hesitant, thinking M may have given her the full rundown on his history of failure. So he resisted the thought.

On the day of the competition, Fred was trimmed, shampooed, and pedicured. He took a picture with Morry and Ben. The competition went smoothly. Fred proved that he could be trained and took second place. Dr. Brown was ecstatic and Morry was proud. This meant that Fred could continue on to the more advanced competitions.

Over the coming months, Fred either placed or showed in each competition he was entered in. He had yet to win, but Dr. Brown reassured Morry that it was just a matter of time.

One day, while Fred was seeing Dr. Brown for a routine visit, the vet mentioned the Platinum Kennel Dog exhibition, the most renowned of all canine competitions. "I don't know, doc. Do you think he's ready?"

"Jack thinks he is. He should know. He says Fred is one of the smartest dogs he's ever trained, and to make up for lost time, he wants to get Fred on the national scene."

Morry smiled. Who would have ever thought that dirty ball of fur, rolling around the streets, would be a dog show competitor?

In preparation for the PKD exhibition, Jack stepped up Fred's training by teaching him other standard maneuvers. Fred and his team, including Morry, were flown out the day before. Fred looked happy and calm, but Morry was a bundle of nerves. You would have thought he was the one wearing the collar.

As Fred performed in each event, he was flawless. When the competition was over, the judges huddled at the table and after much commensuration announced that Best in Show went to Frederico the Pomeranian, owner Morrison Allen, and trainer Jack Jonisen.

Morry cried. He quickly wiped away the tears, not wanting Ben or the other men in his group to see, but it didn't matter since they were crying too, including Dr. Brown.

Fred knew he had done well, and as he took his victory lap around the course, the crowd cheered.

The flight home the next day had a carnival-like atmosphere.

"Morry, the next step is endorsements." Dr. Brown had visions of Fred on every dog product in America.

"Hold on. Let Fred catch his breath!" Morry was laughing. "Right now I just want to get him home and let him rest up a bit."

Fred wagged his tail in agreement. He was on the plane with Morry and the rest of the group. They had chosen to fly on a private jet to avoid transporting Fred like luggage.

Early the next day, at about nine, Morry awakened to find that his cell phone was blowing up! He had ten messages from Dr. Brown, who had started texting him at 8:00 a.m. "Call me, very important!" he read. The same message appeared nine more times.

Morry decided he needed to have his first cup of chocolate-coffee before he spoke with Dr. Brown, just in case it was bad news. Then he called, and steeled himself. "What's up, doc?"

"Guess what?"

"I can't. Why don't you tell me? I'm too tired to guess. I had a late night."

"I got a call from the CEO of Fabulous Feline Frenzy Food Franchise. He saw Fred at the PKD show."

"Yeah, I've heard of them, but they're cat people, hence the name."

"Right, but they want to create a line of dog products featuring Fred. They haven't decided what to call it, but Fred would be on the packaging of all the products, and would even appear in commercials. They're talking a multimillion-dollar deal. You and Fred could be set for life! And I wouldn't be too bad off, either!"

"Sounds good! Get the details, as in the actual contract. I'll think about it. I didn't rescue Fred off of the street just to work him to death."

Dr. Brown emailed a copy of the contract to Morry. After consulting his lawyer, Morry decided that the contract was fair and doable. He also advised Ben that, as a friend to both him and Fred, he would give him 10 percent of the earnings from Fred's contract with Fabulous Feline Frenzy Food Franchise. Ben thought this was too much and only agreed to 5 percent.

After a month of photo shoots and commercials, Fred's part of the deal was done. Fabulous Feline Frenzy Food Franchise took another six months to roll out their canine repertoire. It included dog food and nutrition, dog toys, dog protective wear and a few other product lines. Fred's face appeared on every product. The commercials were cute and clever, often including wordplay of some sort. When the commercial included kids, Fred was made to be cute and cuddly, and when he played opposite adults, Fred was portrayed as sophisticated and worldly. There was something for everyone, and Fred was truly the dog of the hour.

Money was no longer an object, and Fred and Morry were doing well.

Then, one morning, the shoe dropped. Morry heard his doorbell ring. It was early in the morning, about eight o'clock.

A nondescript courier was standing at the door. "Are you Morrison Allen?"

"Yes, I am."

"Sign here." He handed Morry a receipt. "You've just been served!"

Morry almost dropped to his knees. Fred sensed something was wrong and sat at Morry's feet.

Morry read the words carefully. He was being sued by George Foxbourough, Fred's former owner. Foxbourough was claiming ownership of Fred.

Morry called Ben. "That's the most ridiculous thing I've ever heard. First, he chases the dog away. Then he tries to have the dog euthanized. He's just interested in the money. He must have seen Fred on TV. Call your lawyer. He may be able to squash this thing before it gets started."

The next call Morry made was to his lawyer, Lawrence Lawry III. He had been referred to Mr. Lawry by Ben's sister before and had continued to use him for Fred's business.

The next day he went to Mr. Lawry's office with the dreaded document. Morry was absolutely sick at the prospect of losing Fred.

"Can he do this? He let his kids abuse Fred, and then he tried to have Fred euthanized!"

"I don't think he can, but because this is a legal matter, we do have to address it. So let's start by gathering the information that supports your claims of abuse and abandonment."

"Well, when we first started looking for Fred, Mr. Foxbourough advised us that Fred was being dressed up in doll clothing and had sustained pressure sores from being petted by his son too much. Ben can testify to that. Foxbourough also advised the Humane Society to euthanize Fred after refusing to try to keep Fred off the street after he ran away for the second time."

"Well, I'll take a deposition from Ben and the Humane Society. The Society should have a record of Foxbourough's attempt to have Fred euthanized. If we can prove what we all know to be true, we should never have to enter a courtroom," Lawry tried to reassure Morry.

For the next few months, there was a cloud over Morry. Fred could sense something was wrong. He stuck closer to Morry than usual, not sure what was happening. Morry continued to take Fred for walks. He decided to call Maia to see what she was up to these days.

"Hey, I haven't heard from you in a while, Morry. How's Fred?"

"We're both doing fine! Well, actually, we've run into a little snag. Fred's previous owner is trying to get custody of him."

"Really? Well, if there's anything I can do, please let me know."

"Well, can you recall if Foxbourough brought Fred in for treatment of any questionable injuries . . . specifically pressure sores?"

"I don't know. You should check with Dr. Brown."

"Yes, my lawyer has contacted him, but I thought since I had you on the line, I would just check to see what you know."

"I understand. Well, on a more pleasant note, are you still working on your sketches?"

"Only for fun. I've given up on a professional career in art. It's more of a hobby for me now. I'm currently working with the animal rights people."

"That's awesome. Well, if you ever want to grab lunch again, let me know. I hope everything works out for you and Fred!"

"Well what's your schedule like next week?...would you like to go to a movie and dinner?" Morry felt comfortable asking Maia out, since it was her suggestion that they might meet again. This time he would make it a date. After all he now had funds. It would be an event, including flowers. He was planning to make an impression.

"I'd like that. Let me check, my schedule. Friday evening, would probably work best for me. I'll get back to you tomorrow."

Morry continued to get paid for the work Fred performed for Fabulous Feline Frenzy Food Franchise; so neither of them missed any meals. But the stress, of the law suit, was starting to affect Morry's appetite.

One day, while walking Fred, Morry got a call from Lawry. "Good news, Morry. I was able to contact everyone on your list who was familiar with Fred's history with Mr. Foxbourough. It's not perfect, but I have adequate grounds to request a dismissal. Everyone I spoke to supported your assertion that Fred was in an unhealthy environment with Foxbourough. There's no way the judge will take him away from you. The hearing is going to be this afternoon. Because of your deposition, you don't have to be there unless you want to be."

"Okay, Mr. Lawry. Let me know when the hearing is over."

Morry, Ben, and Fred were watching TV when Lawry called back at 1:00 p.m.

"Take a deep breath, Morry. Are you sitting down?"

"Yes, just tell me what I need to know! Did we go down the tubes?"

"No, we prevailed! Booyah! Break out the Moët!"

Morry turned to Ben, who was holding his breath. "Breathe, man! Fred is safe!"

For the first time in the past few months, Morry felt like things were going to be okay. He sat down next to Ben. Fred came and rested in his lap. Morry had finally arrived. He was needed by Fred, and he was where he needed to be!

He smiled, as he recalled, that he had an upcoming date with Maia. Yes, life was looking up.

The Slacker Sisters

CHICAGO

ADVENTURE

GREED

KIDNAPPING

SIBLING RIVALRY

The Slacker Sisters

J ada Johnson was sixty-five years old, but she felt like she was eighty because of the arthritic pain in all of her joints. She had retired early because of the pain and managed to find a good live-in assistant to not only manage her day-to-day household chores, but her business affairs as well. To use an old-school phrase, Laura was her "girl Friday." Her services were expensive, but worth it. After all, she could afford it; she was worth seventy-five million dollars, as of the last accounting. This was the result of selling family stock in a pharmaceutical company her great-grandfather founded many years ago. He had started out as a young pharmacist in a small rural town. After developing and patenting several new medications, he'd been able to raise enough money to start his own company. It had continued to grow in the industry with additional groundbreaking meds that were either manufactured by his company or licensed out to other companies for production.

Jada felt as if she was doing pretty well except for the pain. Ironically, she didn't like taking medications and often resorted to topicals and home remedies for general comfort. She was often asked why. As the previous owner of a pharmaceutical company, many thought she should have been front and center in advocating and using medications for pain relief. People often wondered if she knew something she wasn't telling.

The other issue she didn't know how to take care of was the greed of her granddaughters. She had adopted and raised them after her daughter Gilda had died in a car wreck years before.

Gwyneth was the nicer of the two, but still greedy. Berniece was greedy, lazy, and ruthless, which made her literally dangerous. Both had college degrees, but barely worked. They depended on an allowance from their beloved Grammie, which was what they called Jada, at least to her face.

She was expecting them over today. Gwyneth had advised Jada that they needed to discuss her well-being. Jada knew they were trying to get her into a nursing home. Being of sound mind, she was not going to let this happen, so she was ready for a battle.

At 1:00 p.m. sharp, she heard the bell ring. "Laura, I'm expecting Gwyneth and Berniece for lunch."

"I'll check with the chef to see what we're having."

"Well, it doesn't have to be anything special. They're here more for my money than for lunch."

"What do you mean?"

"They're trying to get me to go to a nursing home so I'll fire you and save money—supposedly their inheritance. But what they don't know is that I'm going to keep you on even while I'm in the home. You're going to watch the little parasites and see what they're up to. You'll also continue to run my personal errands."

As Jada finished speaking to Laura, Jada's maid escorted Gwyneth into the room.

Gwyneth greeted Jada with a perky tone. "Hi, Grammie. You lookin' good today! I brought you a cheese danish from Handler's, the one you love with the raspberry filling in the center."

"Sweetheart, you didn't have to do that. I have plenty of breakfast sweets." What Jada really wanted to say was, "I don't trust you, and I wouldn't eat anything you give me without a forensic analysis." But some things are better left unsaid.

Jada hadn't always felt this way about the granddaughters she'd raised. When they were growing up, she thought they were the sweetest, kindest souls. She gave them whatever they wanted and made sure they were well taken care of after Gilda was killed. Gwyneth had been just three years old and Berniece four years old when it happened. Jada had felt bad for them and tried to make up for the loss of their mother as well as the long hours she spent at the company. She'd probably done too much for them because they'd turned out to be spoiled and lazy. She just hadn't known how spoiled they really were until she'd uncovered Berniece's plan some years before. Apparently Berniece had schemed to have another student take her college entrance exam for her.

Jada had arrived home early and passed by the library door when she'd noticed it was cracked. She had thought Bernie and Gwyn were studying, so she'd proceeded up the stairs, not wanting to break their train of thought.

After putting away her briefcase and coat, she had gone back downstairs to see what they wanted for dinner so the cook could get started. As Grammie had walked in, Berniece had quickly shoved something under her history book.

"What's that Bernie?" Jada had asked her. Gwyn had already left the library.

"Oh, nothing." She'd looked as nervous as a long-tailed cat in a room full of rocking chairs.

"Let me see what you've just shoved under that book."

Reluctantly, Berniece had retrieved Jada's American Express credit card from under her textbook.

"What are you doing with my credit card?!" Jada had been infuriated.

"I just wanted to buy you something for your birthday!"

"My birthday is months away, and why would you use my own card to buy me a gift? You get a generous allowance to buy whatever you want. You're lying and I want the truth, now!"

"I've been studying for my college entrance exam. But the practice questions are just so hard, I don't know if I'll ever be able to pass it!"

"Then what have you been doing for the last four years at that private academy I spent a small fortune to send you to?! And don't try to change the subject. I still want to know what you're doing with my credit card."

"That's what I'm trying to tell you. Clarice promised to take the exam for me if I bought her a Birkin bag, but I don't have that kind of money."

"And neither do I." Jada had snatched the card from Berniece's sweaty hands and placed it in the pocket of her slacks. She had realized then that she was going to have to start locking her valuables up. She had been so disappointed in her granddaughter. Not only had she been hurt, but she'd wondered how she could have raised such a selfish brat!

Then it occurred to her: she hadn't raised her granddaughters at all. During grammar school and high school, they'd spent their evenings with staff while she tended to work she had brought home from the office. On weekends, she'd offered to spend time with them, but they'd opted to hang out with their friends instead. Now, years later, Jada could see that because she didn't put in the time with Berniece and Gwyneth, she had nothing to show for it.

From that point on, there had been a rift between her and her granddaughters. While she had never been in direct conflict with Gwyn, Gwyn had formed an unspoken alliance with Berniece, and now it was them against her, especially if it was important. They both went away to college and got a BS in liberal arts, but nothing of any consequence. It soon became obvious to Jada that their only goals in life were to receive their yearly allowance of $125,000 and wait for her to die to get the rest.

After Berniece stole Jada's American Express, there was no going back. They were civil to each other, but Jada knew she couldn't trust Berniece, or Gwyn for that matter. They both had very little moral character or integrity. If there was any question about how they felt about her, it was made crystal clear when she overheard Berniece discussing her on the day of her high school graduation ceremony.

Jada had been looking for Berniece, to bring her the cap and gown she'd left in Jada's car. Just as she had walked up to the pre-commencement grounds, she'd heard a group of girls laughing. She'd recognized Berniece's saccharine voice as she had drawn within earshot and heard, "Yeah, that's right. The old wretch can't keep up with her own checkbook. That's how I was able to steal a few checks and forge her signature. She doesn't even know it's missing. By the time she gets the statements back, it'll be too late. Besides, she won't even know it was me."

Jada had stopped dead in her tracks, unable to believe the words streaming out of her granddaughter's mouth. When the others had stopped laughing, Berniece had whirled around, utterly dumbfounded. All this time, Gwyn had been pulling on her sleeve, but Berniece had been too wrapped up in the moment to heed the warning.

Jada had dropped the cap and gown and walked away. The rest of the day was a blur. She had planned a whole day of activities for Berniece that included a reception and gifts, even a car that Berniece had begged for through all four years of high school. But then Jada had wished she could take it all back. Well, at least she'd discovered where she stood. She'd performed the same ritual for Gwyn the following year, but that was all it was, a ritual. Jada's heart hadn't been in it and things would never be the same.

Now, as Gwyn sat down, the doorbell chimed again. "That must be Bernie. She said she'd be a few minutes late. She wanted to stop and get you your favorite cappuccino!"

Jada's thoughts returned to the present.

Jada didn't say anything, but she wasn't any more likely to drink the cappuccino than she was to eat Gwyn's danish.

"Hi, Grammie!" Berniece rushed to kiss Jada on the cheek. Jada turned to her with apprehension as though being approached by a snake. "Here's your favorite cappuccino!" Berniece continued. "Sorry I'm late, but there was a long line, and then I got caught in traffic."

"Never mind. The important thing is that you're here. Now, let's get down to business. The two of you have some misguided thought that I would be better off in a nursing home. Most of the facilities are limited in resources and have inadequate help. I've looked into them. The only way I'll go into a nursing home is if I choose the facility. Also, you girls would have to volunteer two days a week at that facility."

"Now, Grammie," Berniece smiled, gritting her teeth at the same time. "You know Gwyn and I have things we need to do. We couldn't possibly do that!"

"It wouldn't be so bad," Gwyn countered. Berniece rolled her eyes at Gwyn to show her disapproval, a gesture that wasn't lost on Jada. Berniece was the obvious leader between the two.

Gwyn was one year younger than Berniece, but appeared to be much younger. When she wasn't around Berniece, Gwyn

225

had presence. When Berniece appeared, Gwyn faded into the background like wallpaper.

"All I meant to say was that it would be like volunteering for charity, which we've done before! But if Berniece thinks it's a bad idea—" Her voice was high-pitched and apologetic.

"It doesn't matter what she thinks! I'm setting the terms of this arrangement, and I will determine how long it goes on. In essence, this is an experiment. I set the terms, and I can change my mind at any time." Jada was tired of being harassed and intended to prove to these two loafers that putting her in a home wasn't going to solve their problems.

"We're only thinking of you, Grammie. After all, you're here all alone in this big house. It would be fun to be around others your own age . . . people to talk to and socialize with, and staff to help you with all your needs!" Berniece went on the offensive while trying to appear to be thoughtful.

"I have all of those things here. I have a full staff. Laura is a great assistant. I have a cook and a driver. I have friends who visit. I have hobbies, and I'm in clubs. The two of you want me to think you're trying to keep me from a dismal existence, but that's not true. Let's talk about the elephant that's not only in the room, but running all around it! Money, money, money— that's all it's ever been." Jada was no longer trying to hide her anger. "The two of you have never worked a day in your lives. I thought sending you to private schools and the best colleges would help build your character. You've never had to work for anything, and you've squandered every opportunity to make your own way in life."

"When the two of you were younger and your mother passed away, I was initially overwhelmed with the thought of

226

having to raise the two of you. But then the prospect of raising two warrior princesses intrigued and challenged me. I thought I was going to groom you to take over the business. You may not remember, but in the summers, I used to take you to the office every Monday to show you what I did for a living. You were about nine or ten years old.

"Gwyn, you seemed to enjoy product development and wanted to hang out in the pilot lab. I thought, at the very least, you might become a pharmacist or chemist. Berniece, you would sneak off and hide in the bathroom . . . and I say 'hide', but you weren't fooling anyone. I knew where you were. So eventually, I just left you at home with Freda, the maid. At some point, Gwyn, your interest in the lab dissipated, and you both declined any further company involvement. By then, you were both in high school, and I had no intention of trying to steer you into something that you clearly had no interest in."

Convicted of their own greed, the two young women just sat there, stunned by the direct speech of their grandmother, who for the most part was usually restrained.

"Grammie, we love you," Gwyn whimpered, trying to soften the moment. Berniece only sat in silence, thinking thoughts that did not include Jada's well-being.

Ignoring the last sentiment, Jada proceeded. "I've chosen to move into Cedar Palace Nursing Facility and Rehab Center. While it's not perfect, I can get the rehabilitative services that you all claim you want me to have. It's close to my real home, and after a month we'll see if I want to continue to live there. To this end, I will continue to maintain the same staff and residence here until I make a decision."

With this last revelation, Berniece's mouth fell wide open, revealing the wad of gum that she had recently popped into it. This meant that Jada was going to be spending twice as much money as she was spending now, if not more. She and Gwyn hadn't figured on Jada maintaining her mansion while living in a nursing home. But they knew better than to object, for fear that it could be worse. After all, she might cut them out of her will, if she hadn't already.

In a conversation a month before, Laura had suggested to Jada that she could disinherit her granddaughters and leave her money to a deserving charity.

"I've thought of that, Laura, but it would break my heart to disinherit Gilda's daughters. When she died, I promised myself that they would never lack for anything. Their father literally dropped them on my doorstep, stating that he couldn't take care of two daughters by himself. He left and never looked back. So, to leave them out of my will would seem like total abandonment. But I agree—they don't deserve an inheritance. They've never worked for anything, and have never wanted for anything, and as a result, they aren't worth anything! But I'm going to make one last effort to salvage any character that might be left in them!"

"How do you propose to do that?"

"Well, they want me in a nursing home. So I'll go, with the stipulation that they volunteer there two days a week. As a resident, I'll be able to see what kind of job they're doing. I also plan to make any future allowances and inheritance contingent upon their continued participation at the home and a good evaluation by the manager."

"That's a tall order for girls who have never worked a day in their lives."

"Exactly, and at twenty-three and twenty-four years old, they need to start learning responsibility. Two days a week of volunteer work will still be a bargain, considering their allowance and what they stand to inherit!"

When Jada had this conversation with Laura, she knew springing this on her granddaughters was not going to be easy, but she was determined to try.

Now that she'd broken the news to them, Jada paused to get their reaction. With Berniece's mouth open wide enough to catch flies, she knew she had struck a nerve. Because Berniece was speechless, Gwyn didn't know how to react.

"That's right. I'm going to maintain my home while I'm in this nursing home to determine if it's a good fit. The two of you will not only volunteer there two days a week, but if you fail to do so, I'll cut off your allowance and your inheritance."

"Whaaaaat?!" Berniece and Gwyn responded in unison, as if sharing the same brain.

"As incredible as this might sound, let me put it into context for you. I don't know of any job in America, or in any country, for that matter, where you can work two days a week without any special talent and get paid $125,000 a year. So you can take it or leave it!"

There was no response. Gwyn looked as if someone had sucker-punched her in the gut and Berniece looked angry enough to bite a snake.

"I'll take your silence as a yes. You need to report to the Cedar Palace manager bright and early on Monday at 8:00 a.m. He'll give you your roles and assignments. And as we working people would say, 'Have a good weekend!'" Jada smiled with finality.

Both young women stormed out. Berniece snatched up her cappuccino from the coffee table before she left.

Laura mused, "They didn't bother to stay for lunch."

"Yeah, I guess they lost their appetites!"

"What do you want me to do with this danish?"

"Throw it away, unless you're brave enough to eat it!" Jada said half-jokingly, but with enough conviction that Laura immediately disposed of it.

That Monday, 8:00 a.m. arrived, and so did 8:30 a.m. and 9:00 a.m. But Berniece and Gwyn didn't arrive until 9:30 a.m. Upon signing in, they were escorted to the office of Mr. Gilchrist, the manager. After bringing the sisters in, the secretary walked out, but stood outside the door within earshot. This was going to be some tongue-lashing, and she wouldn't miss it for the world.

She wasn't disappointed.

"I don't know what you all plan to do going forward, but volunteers start at 8:00 a.m., the same as our regular employees. We have a job to do, and our residents depend on us to get it done. If you can't adhere to this, don't bother to come back. I understand that you all will be giving us two days a week. But, please, don't become more trouble than you're worth! Follow me while I take you to your team lead to get your assignment schedule."

Berniece and Gwyn were impressed with the modern facility. Grammie had chosen well. This was a good place. The hallways were wide, the rooms were clean, and there were no foul odors wafting through the corridors or patients calling out in pain. The employees had on uniforms that were starched and clean. This was a class act. What they didn't know was that Jada had bought this nursing home the year before and implemented changes to make it a state-of-the art-facility. The kitchen served cuisine that was nutritionally sound and customized for each resident based on their morbidities.

Gwyn was pleased, but Berniece wasn't. There was no way Grammie would succumb to the general ills that occur in some nursing homes in a place like this. Berniece's general plan to get Jada into a nursing home was not only to keep her from spending excess money on in-home services, but to put her in harm's way. Berniece had seen many commercials for lawyers looking for victims of nursing home abuse. So what were the odds that Grammie would actually find a home of this caliber? Who even knew such a place existed?

As if to answer this question, Mr. Gilchrist dropped a bombshell. "Before your grandmother bought Cedar Palace, it was deplorable. The building was in disrepair, the services were substandard, and the food was awful. She hired contractors to renovate the building, and then she upgraded the services and hired new staff. The residents love her. She has acquired saint status around here!"

Berniece silently cursed her grandmother. How dare she squander funds needed to support my future? screamed the thoughts of entitlement that raced through Berniece's head.

Gwyn, on the other hand, wasn't as concerned. Grammie had done a good thing. Surely there would still be enough money for all of them to continue to live comfortably. All she needed to do was to give two days a week to people less able than herself.

Their first assignment was to rotate through the rehab department. The lead technician gave them a tour of the department, detailing the function and safety features of each piece of equipment. They were to clean the equipment first thing in the morning and after each resident's use. As they became more familiar with the department, they would assist with the actual training itself.

"Wow, this is exciting! I can't wait to get started." Gwyn had never had a job and couldn't contain her enthusiasm.

Berniece looked at Gwyn in disgust. This little idiot couldn't see what the old lady was doing. She was spending all their inheritance right before their eyes, and there was nothing they could do about it.

At 4:00 p.m., the end of their first day, Bernie was fuming. As she and Gwyn got into the car, she could hardly contain her anger. "Don't you see what she's doing? Are you that dense? She's spending our inheritance on a nursing home that's going to consume more money than it will ever make. By the time she dies, we'll be penniless, living on the street, fighting wild dogs for food. Or, worse yet, we may actually have to work for a living. We have to do something!"

"I don't know that that's true, Bernie. I feel pretty good about what Grammie has done. Actually, I'm proud. I didn't think I would like volunteering, but if this works out, I may want to do it more than just two days a week."

"Oh, now you're just talking crazy. Who wants to work at a nursing home?"

The wheels in Berniece's brain were turning. The old lady must have lost her marbles. That's it, Berniece thought. Have her committed and get control of the money. But how to go about it?

First she would consult a professional. The next day, during her volunteer lunch break, she called Dr. Blake. She had seen Dr. Blake several years before, when she'd suffered a bout of depression.

"Hi, Dr. Blake. This is Bernie Johnson. I saw you about a year ago for depression. But now I'm concerned about my grandmother. She's spending money indiscriminately, and I'm concerned that she's suffering from dementia. I want you to evaluate her."

"I would like to help your grandmother, but if you truly think she's demented, take her to a neurologist. They're better equipped to deal with this matter. Hang on while my staff gets the number for you." Berniece held the line and quietly waited.

She had tried to get Gwyneth involved.

Gwyn, however, had drunk the Kool-Aid, and she wasn't going back. "Grammie is not demented. She's as sharp as ever. She's just trying to do something good!"

The next day, Gwyn called Jada to let her know about Berniece's plan.

"Grammie, I don't understand why she's so angry. I'm confident that what you're doing is right. I'll admit that when you first presented the idea of volunteering at a nursing home, I thought you were off your game. But after two weeks there, I'm seeing the good that's being done for the residents and I like it! It makes me feel good!"

"That's good, Gwyn, because I'll be moving into Cedar Palace in the next month or so, per our discussion."

"Yes, I think you'll like living there, at least for thirty days, if not longer. But Grammie, I really called to warn you. Bernie is going to try to have you diagnosed with dementia to get control of your money."

"Thanks for the warning, but there's nothing wrong with me that a good Tom Collins and a foot massage won't help!" They both laughed. It was like old times, before Berniece had turned Gwyn against her. It looked like Gwyn was starting to use her own brain for a change.

"Don't worry, Gwyn. I'll take care of it."

After hanging up, Jada immediately called her lawyer. She needed to be prepared for anything the bottom feeder might throw her way. She knew Berniece was ruthless, but she hadn't expected her to go to these extremes to get her money.

"Hi, Ms. Johnson. What can I do for you?"

"Mr. Lawry, my own flesh and blood has turned against me. My granddaughter is trying to gain control of my estate by declaring that I am demented."

"No worries. We both know you have one of the sharpest minds this side of heaven. But we're going to go on the offensive. I want you to go to your personal MD and have a routine annual physical exam, including a mental and cognitive status evaluation. That way if she challenges your mental capacity, she won't have a leg to stand on. In the meantime, I can write her out of your will!"

"Well, I was hoping I wouldn't have to disinherit her. She is my granddaughter, after all."

"Yes, and as long as she stands to inherit any part of your estate, she's a threat to you. She has proven that she'll go to extreme lengths to get your money. You also need to let her know that she's out of your will so there will be no incentive for her to harm you physically or slander you with accusations of being demented."

As difficult as Berniece was to deal with, Jada still wasn't ready to write her off. Maybe she would come around like Gwyn. What Jada discounted was that although Bernie and Gwyn were sisters, Berniece just didn't have the same heart as Gwyn.

As the month progressed, Berniece became more incensed as she saw Cedar Palace improvements continuing to be made with "her money."

By the end of the month, Jada had moved into Cedar Palace. She was taking full advantage of the amenities and services to make sure they were up to the standards she had set as the new owner.

Gwyn and Berniece continued to come to the home two days a week. Gwyn even wanted to increase her volunteer time.

"Just remember," Jada warned, "your allowance isn't going to increase just because you've increased your time at Cedar Palace. You're already being paid well above any other employee's compensation! And we have an agreement!"

"Yeah, Grammie, but I'm not an employee." She smiled.

Jada smiled as well. They were on much better terms these days, and Jada could feel the warmth they'd had before Berniece had come between them years ago.

"Also, Grammie, I'd like to find out how to become an assistant manager."

"Well, first you'd have to become an employee. Second, you'd need to get formal training and go through a development program. We can discuss the details later."

Jada Johnson was all about business. Although she was proud of Gwyn's initiative in wanting to become more involved at Cedar Palace, Gwyn needed to go through the same process as any other employee. Loyalty wouldn't be enough; she would need to prove that she was able to do the job. She had been under volunteer status throughout her time there. Blood might be thicker than water, but . . . Jada let that thought go as she heard someone knocking at her door.

"Come in."

Mr. Gilchrist rushed in, obviously flustered.

"We've got a problem. There are picketers out front, with signs protesting unfair working conditions at Cedar Palace."

"Why would that be? I've upgraded this facility with the latest equipment and a gym and new cafeteria for the staff. Also, I increased everyone's salary by 15 percent with the purchase."

"That's just it! I know all our staff. No one in that picket line is a current employee, and all our personnel are present and accounted for. This is designed to make either the facility look bad, or you personally. I'm going to deal with the media. Crews are starting to gather outside, and bad press isn't something we can afford within the first few months of reorganizing and changing our image! But you need to find out where this is coming from and nip it in the bud."

Jada knew immediately where it had come from. Today was not a volunteer day for Berniece, but she knew exactly where to find her. Jada called for her driver. As they arrived at the Olive Verde Door Spa and Salon, Jada jumped out before the Maybach could come to a complete stop. Striding past the front desk, she immediately headed to the back of the spa.

The front desk clerk came running, after her. "Miss! Miss, you can't go back there without an appointment! Come back before I call security."

Jada turned around to face the young clerk, who immediately recognized her as a VIP customer and board member. "Sorry, Ms. Johnson, I didn't recognize you! Are you looking for someone?"

"No. I know exactly where I'm going!" Jada proceeded down the corridor leading to the locker room, and from there, directly into the mud room.

Berniece was completely covered in rare earth mud, with cucumbers over each eye, and sipping celery-infused water. As soon as the door opened, she knew it was Jada because of the familiar scent of her specialty cologne.

"Ah, the smell of money. I'd know it anywhere! My dear Grammie, what brings you here today? I thought your spa day was Thursday." The sarcasm dripped from every syllable that left Berniece's lurid lips.

"You know why I'm here! What is the meaning of that phony protest outside Cedar Palace?"

"I can't help it if your employees don't like the way you conduct business or your management style!"

"Just how stupid do you think I am? Or better yet, how stupid are you?" Before Berniece could respond, Jada continued. "Anything that affects that nursing home directly affects the value of your inheritance. So if you think you're hurting me when you try to undermine this investment, you're only partially right. If the nursing home fails, the financial loss is going to decrease your inheritance, as well as Gwyn's. But I'll make sure you take the brunt of it, seeing as how it will be because of you."

Berniece sat bolt upright and the cucumbers fell to the floor. "I thought I was disinherited!"

After Berniece's failed attempt to have her declared incompetent, Mr. Lawry had advised her to write Berniece out of her will, but Jada was still trying to hold on to family. This was what her grandfather had told her father as the company was passed down to him: "Always hold on to family. At the end of the day, that's all we have!" This credo was starting to wear thin. After all, granddaddy had never had to deal with the likes of Berniece.

"No, I haven't written you out of the will, but after what you did today, I'm starting to rethink that decision."

"I'm sorry, Grammie! I didn't mean to hurt you personally. I was just so upset when you bought Cedar Palace without discussing it with us. That wasn't the plan. You were to move into a home, not buy it as well. I'll do better. Just give me a second chance!" Berniece mustered all the fake humility she could, trying to sound convincing.

"First off, it's my money—not yours! I do with it as I please, and not until I take my last breath do you have any say in that. I'll think about what I'm going to do about your last little stunt, but in the meantime, you'd better call off the low-class riffraff that are picketing at Cedar Palace!"

Berniece still wasn't admitting she'd hired the fake protesters, but when Jada arrived back at the nursing home, they were gone.

That evening, Jada called Lawry. "Hi, Lawrence. Berniece pulled another stunt today. So I've decided to decrease her part of the inheritance to 10 percent. Gwyn will still get her 50 percent, and the other 40 percent, I'm giving to charity. When you've drafted the changes, just send it by courier. I'll have it notarized and returned."

"Jada, are you not afraid of her? She's been nothing but trouble since you took her in years ago. Did you ever consider that maybe their dad knew something you didn't know when he abandoned them on your doorstep twenty years ago?"

Jada laughed. "Lawrence, you're so melodramatic, I feel as if I'm in some dark thriller!"

"All I'm saying is watch your back. She's becoming more aggressive as she gets older. She's lazy and she's greedy, and you have no idea if there are any limits to what she'll do."

"Well, make the changes, and we'll see how things unfold. Talk to ya later." Jada ended the call feeling apprehensive. Lawry had always thought it was a bad idea to tell Berniece and Gwyn too much about the family fortune. He also felt that she was too generous with their allowance. Maybe he was right!

The next two weeks were uneventful. Jada was pleased with Mr. Gilchrist's management skills. She could tell that the fiasco Bernice had planned didn't work. He had gotten out in front of what could have been an embarrassment and squashed it in the press. Also, the fact that the picketers left shortly after Jada confronted Berniece confirmed to the press that there was smoke, but no fire.

Jada herself was feeling better thanks to the rehab program she was undergoing for her rheumatoid arthritis. She still had the deformities, which would never go away, but the pain was so much better. Some days, she didn't notice the pain at all. It had been a month since she'd entered Cedar Palace, and she had decided to stay. She would still maintain her mansion a little longer.

Gwyn had brought her several postgraduate business brochures on long-term care management. It appeared that she was taking this seriously. However, Jada wasn't holding her breath; she needed to see if Gwyn would continue to volunteer after the newness of her experience at the home wore off. At least she had embraced the experience, something Bernice never did. Berniece continued to be resentful of the two days a week she had to spend there.

One day, Jada decided to go for a day of shopping downtown. She advised William, her driver, that she would need him all day. Her car was parked in the Cedar Palace lot. When William arrived in his own private car, he thought he saw some liquid beneath the Maybach, but he assumed that it had already been there when he'd parked Jada's car the day before. Starting the car up, William called Jada. "I'm downstairs. I'll pull around the front in ten minutes to pick you up." The lot was on an incline, so as he pulled out of the back entrance and circled the building, there was some natural acceleration, but he didn't bother to try to slow down since he was able to control the car. By the time he arrived around front, there was no Jada. Instead, Berniece was stepping off of the curb with her back turned. He pressed on the brakes, but nothing happened. He frantically pumped the brakes, still with no response. By then he was honking his horn for Berniece to move. She turned around just in time to see the car before it ran over her. William, unable to stop the car, dove out of it. It continued to careen down the hill until it hit a tree and stalled.

"William, are you okay?" Jada had just arrived on the scene. "Someone call 911!"

"I'm okay, but what about Berniece?" William was rubbing his head.

Jada frantically turned around to see her granddaughter unconscious on the ground. She initially didn't see her on the pavement since she had only expected to see William as she encountered the car rolling down the street.

"Bernie! Bernie! Say something! Are you okay?!" Bernie groaned, but nothing intelligible passed her lips. Soon an ambulance arrived on the scene and took both Bernie and William away.

Inspection of the car by the police later determined that the brake line had been cut.

William surmised that the fluid he'd seen on the ground before he got into the car must have been brake fluid. But why would someone do that, he wondered?

He didn't have to wonder long. Berniece, who suffered a spinal injury, admitted to cutting the brake line. This was after her doctors determined that the injury had left her a paraplegic. They didn't hold out much hope for even a partial recovery.

"Do you want to press charges, Ms. Johnson? After all, that was pretty malicious." The police came to Jada after questioning Berniece in the hospital some days later.

"No, I think being paralyzed the rest of her young life will be punishment enough." Jada walked in to see Berniece, who had her head turned toward the wall. She had heard Jada outside and didn't want to talk to her.

"Bernie, I'm sorry you got hurt! But when they first told me that you admitted to cutting the brake line on my car, I couldn't believe it. What were you thinking?" Bernice never responded or turned to face Jada. Jada walked out.

Jada and Gwyn came to the hospital every day for the next few weeks as Bernice went through inpatient rehab. Dr. Ben Kasey was compassionate but direct when he told them, "There's very little hope that she'll ever walk again. However, there's nothing to keep you from praying for a miracle. You should also look for a good nursing home since she'll need intense supportive care the first few weeks. I hear Cedar Palace is good. They've just recently been renovated, their equipment is cutting edge, and the staff is excellent!"

Jada beamed. She decided not to tell Dr. Kasey that she owned Cedar Palace. The fact that it had such a good reputation was enough for her!

CHICAGO

ADVENTURE

GREED

KIDNAPPING

SIBLING RIVALRY

www.ingramcontent.com/pod-product-compliance
Lightning Source LLC
Chambersburg PA
CBHW070749280626
47162CB00018B/2814